THE GUNS OF HAMMER

THE GUNS OF HAMMER

Barry Cord

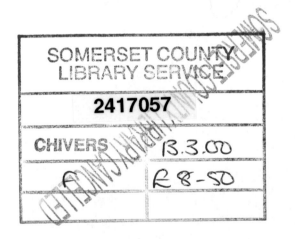

Chivers Press   G.K. Hall & Co.
Bath, England • Thorndike, Maine USA

This Large Print edition is published by Chivers Press, England, and by G.K. Hall & Co., USA.

Published in 1999 in the U.K. by arrangement with the author, care of Golden West Literary Agency.

Published in 1999 in the U.S. by arrangement with Golden West Literary Agency.

U.K. Hardcover   ISBN 0-7540-3749-5   (Chivers Large Print)
U.K. Softcover   ISBN 0-7540-3750-9   (Camden Large Print)
U.S. Softcover   ISBN 0-7838-8580-6   (Nightingale Series Edition)

The text of this Large Print edition is unabridged.
Other aspects of the book may vary from the original edition.

Set in 16 pt. New Times Roman.

Printed in Great Britain on acid-free paper.

British Library Cataloguing in Publication Data available

Library of Congress Cataloging-in-Publication Data

Cord, Barry, 1913–
    The guns of Hammer / Barry Cord.
       p.   cm.
    ISBN 0-7838-8580-6 (lg. print : sc : alk. paper)
    1. Large type books. I. Title.
    [PS3505.O6646G86   1999]
    813'.54—dc21   99–19637

CHAPTER ONE

Kate Barrow saw the rider swing into view at the far end of Jackson Street, and even though it was night she recognized the bulk of the man against the low-hanging stars.

She stopped, a little gasp escaping her. The man at her side said: 'Miles?' and at her quick nod he touched her arm, half in defiance. 'He's got to know sometime, Kate—'

'No—no—' She turned and looked up into Ned Atwell's shadowed face. 'Not now. Please, Ned? He hasn't seen us. If you'll—'

Ned Atwell, tall and slender and handsome in town clothes, nodded resignedly 'It isn't fair to Miles,' he muttered, 'nor to me. I'm his friend, too, Kate. But in things like this—'

Her fingers tightened on his arm. 'Please!' she breathed.

He shrugged. 'I'll call on your father tomorrow?' His tone held a bitter wryness.

She nodded quickly. 'Yes—yes!'

He turned and glanced back to the saloon two doors away. 'I need a drink anyway,' he murmured. 'Good night, Kate.'

Kate didn't look back. She kept walking until she reached the corner. The big rider saw her then and pulled in to the walk.

'Miles!' she said, forcing surprise into her voice. 'How nice. I didn't expect you in town tonight.'

Miles North stepped out of saddle and came up to the walk. He loomed over her by a head—a big man, hard and solid and unsmiling. She glimpsed his face and sensed the violence in this man she had consented to marry; a violence which both repelled and attracted her.

'Sorry, Kate,' he said softly. He was always gentle with her, always correct. He held himself in leash with her. She knew this, and sometimes it frightened her.

'Miles—I was just going home. Dad will be glad to see you.'

He shook his head. 'Not tonight. I'm in town on other business. But I will walk you home.'

She was slim and poised, her voice was soft, and there was a smell of sweet lilacs about her that suggested fragility. She didn't belong in this valley cowtown only one step from frontier roughness, and he wondered again what had brought Major John Barrow and his daughter to Chuckline.

Kate hesitated. 'If you want to, Miles,' she assented. She would never oppose him. She knew it and she hated herself for it.

Miles North stepped off the walk to the big black waiting in the street. A swirl of sand ran like a puff of smoke down the almost deserted road—the grit rustled onto the boardwalk like the soft slithering of a snake. Kate Barrow turned her face from the stinging wind.

Miles looped his reins around the black's pommel. 'Follow along, Mig,' he said softly. The black tossed his head in understanding.

He joined the girl on the walk, took her arm. For a bare moment he paused, his glance searching the shadows up the street, and Kate felt the grim expectancy in him. She said quickly: 'Miles—if you really must see someone on business—'

'It can wait,' he said shortly.

He turned down Sawyer Street with her, and almost immediately they left Chuckline's business district. A crossroads town on the edge of the desert, it would never be anything else. Miles was silent as he walked with this girl under the shadowing cottonwoods to the Barrow cottage

Kate's light chatter about the coming church social fell apart under the press of Miles' silence. They walked the last fifty yards in silence, only the big black's trailing hoofs making a sound in the dry, rustling night.

He stopped at the small gate, opened it for her. She turned and looked up at him and instinctively froze as he put his big hands on her shoulders and bent to kiss her. He felt her withdrawal, and his kiss was light and brief.

'Good night, Kate,' he said. 'I'll see you later in the week.'

He turned and walked back, the black trailing after him. Kate waited a moment before going into the house. She felt small and miserable and unhappy. She had promised to marry this man, and she didn't love him . . .

*   *   *

Miles North came back to the corner of Jackson and Sawyer and waited, his restless glance probing the shadows. The leashed expectancy stirred in him as a small figure shuffled into a patch of light on the opposite walk, paused a moment to pick him out, then headed for him.

A fiddle wailed plaintively inside the Casa Grande at Miles' back—from one of the upstairs rooms a man's rough voice lashed out, riding down a woman's query. The tinder dryness of this land, forty days without rain, gave an edgy atmosphere to the town, and tempers were short and ugly.

The small figure loomed up in front of Miles and became a weatherbeaten man of some fifty years, shapeless in old range clothes, sagging cartridge belt, battered gray Stetson. He stepped up to the walk and said shortly: 'He's in Charlie's—' and fell in step with the younger man as Miles wheeled abruptly away.

They walked without conversation. The small man was Miles' foreman, twice Miles' age and half his size—and long on silence. He quickened his steps to keep up with the younger man's stride, his grizzled jaws working methodically on a quid of tobacco.

4

Miles North was a big man; a rangy, long-muscled man with a stubborn jaw and a line of bitterness that ran down from his gray eyes to the hard crimp of his mouth. He headed for Charlie's, high heels hitting the boards solidly, and when he reached the low adobe building with CHARLIE'S BAR painted across the dirty windows, he turned and palmed the batwings open.

Cud Walker, his foreman, hesitated in the doorway, a tight grin on his usually sour face. Behind him a group of cow ponies moved restlessly against the rail.

Three drinkers were hunched over the far end of the small bar. A bigger group gathered quietly around a card table in the rear of the room, directly under an overhead oil lamp.

Miles wheeled toward this group while Cud Walker drifted slowly toward the shadowed wall. This was Miles' play and he knew the temper of the man who now ran the Hammer spread.

The relaxed atmosphere in Charlie's changed with Miles' entrance, as if someone had rammed a charge of giant powder into the room and lighted the fuse. The three drinkers eased back along the bar, turning to keep a watchful eye on the big man walking toward the card players. Charlie's man, Terry, a small, thin-faced oldster with nervous hands, slid back toward a rear room. Terry always went for Charlie when trouble brewed.

5

The men at the card table kept playing. But the easy banter that had marked their game fell off and faces were suddenly impassive in the yellow lamp glow.

Miles looked them over, a contemptuous twist to his lips. There were Mike O'Lean, Joe Larsen, Shorty Baker, 'Dutch' Muehler and Benjamin Gaines. The first four he had known most of his life; they had been his father's friends. Benjamin Gaines was new. All of them, including Gaines, were men with small outfits; farmers who ran a few cattle south of Miles' big Hammer spread.

Gaines had bought the Pothole from Canady's widow, moved in with a hired hand and started to expand. There was only one way he could expand—onto Hammer grass.

Miles' hard gaze singled him out. 'You, Gaines!' he snapped. 'I told you to keep your cows off the Strip!'

Gaines looked up then, a red flush staining his heavy neck. He was about Miles' age, half a foot shorter and ten pounds heavier; a sandy-haired, solid man, slow to move but hard to stop once in motion. Of the group around the table he alone wore a belt gun.

He said carefully, picking his words, 'I don't want trouble with you, Miles.' He repeated it, reading the anger burning hot in the other's eyes. 'I don't want trouble with you—'

'Then run your cows off the Strip!' Miles said flatly. 'And keep them off Hammer grass!'

6

He swung around then, his gaze holding the others around the table, challenging them individually. 'That goes for all of you. Stay clear of Hammer grass!'

Mike O'Lean shifted restlessly. He was a small, wiry, bitter man, tied down by a wife and five small children. He had come into the valley only a year after old Farnum North had founded Chuckline, when this town had been nothing but a general store at a trail crossing. A young, handsome man with ambition, he had married too early and his bitterness had increased in direct ratio to the success of the men who had come after him.

Mike had tried his hand at half a dozen ventures, and they had folded. Now all ambition had been sucked out of him, leaving him an embittered and dangerous man.

'The Strip's open range,' he pointed out. 'You can't keep us off, Miles. You know it has the only waterhole in ten miles—'

'And barely enough water for Hammer beef!' Miles snapped. 'Not enough for every two-bit rancher who suddenly decides he wants to spread out—at Hammer's expense!'

Mike's fingers crushed his cards. Shorty Baker laid a restraining hand on his arm. Shorty was a mild, chunky man with straw hair, blue eyes and a smile that weathered anger, hate and disappointment.

'Your dad was an understanding man, Miles. When the dry spells came, he helped us little

7

fellas out.'

'My father was a soft man,' Miles said harshly. 'But I remember when you used to ask him to use the Strip's water, not try to crowd Hammer beef out!'

Shorty looked uncomfortable and glanced at Gaines. Ben sneered. 'The lot of us have kowtowed too long before Hammer,' he growled.

Miles' eyes held small wicked lights. 'You speaking for all the boys, Ben—'

Shorty added quickly, 'Miles, we knew you since you were knee high, before you went East to that medical school. You ain't the same man who left here a year ago—' His voice faltered, petered out.

Miles was eyeing Gaines, separating the thick-necked man from the others at the table. His voice had a metallic ring. 'I came looking for you,' he said, 'because I heard you've been saying I needed a lesson. You want to be the teacher?'

Gaines swallowed. The others around the table stiffened, and no one heard Charlie come into the room, followed by Terry.

Miles loomed over Gaines, his face dark and watchful, and there was no softness in him, no relenting.

'Well?'

A red stain crept up Gaines' thick neck. His eyes held an uncertain flicker.

'Canady said he allus ran his beef onto Strip

8

water,' he mumbled. 'You got no right—'

'You ain't Canady!' Miles cut him off. 'I don't know you, Gaines. I don't know what you're after. But if it's trouble you want, you're headed in the right direction.' Miles' eyes took in the others at the card table. 'Mebbe this loudmouth talked you boys into believing that, with Dad gone, Hammer would be an easy touch. He's wrong. You keep listening to him and you'll find out just how wrong you are!'

O'Lean moved restlessly. The others stood quiet, faces harsh in the lamplight.

'I'm warning you this last time,' Miles said, speaking directly to Gaines. 'Keep your cows off the Strip!'

He waited a moment, conscious of the sullen temper in the man; knowing that this man was part of Hammer's troubles; wondering, too, if he fitted into the puzzle of his father's disappearance.

Benjamin Gaines was a newcomer to the valley. It was odd that he had come in to take over Canady's small spread only a few weeks after Farnum North rode north, toward Saddle Pass—and disappeared.

Miles waited, holding his violence in check with an effort. Gaines kept his eyes on the cards in his hands, and finally Miles murmured: 'I figured you was all mouth, Gaines!'

The thick-necked man's temper ignited then. He turned his head, blurted thickly: 'You

9

go to the devil, Miles!'

CHAPTER TWO

Miles was turning away when Gaines said that. He wheeled back, leaned over the table and backhanded Gaines across the mouth. Gaines grunted and heaved erect, pushing the table out of his way like an angry grizzly, and Miles hit him.

It was a savage punch, thrown with all the pent-up violence in him, and he felt his knuckles crack against Gaines' skull. Pain shot up Miles' right arm, twisting a snarl from his tight lips. All the driving anger in him, scraped raw by the hot dry winds, by sleepless nights, by the dozen and one things which had been plaguing Hammer since his father's disappearance, exploded in his driving fists.

Gaines was falling back and the others were scrambling clear of the table when Miles shoved O'Lean aside and went after the big farmer. He hit Gaines in the face with his left and brought his right across again, his rage acting as an anesthetic, dulling the pain. Gaines' bloody face loomed up and he closed in, his thick arms going around Miles' waist. His weight drove Miles back against the bar, shaking it. All of Gaines' enormous strength went into that hug as he tried to break Miles' back.

Miles pulled his injured hand free and thrust it into Gaines' distorted face. His fingers dug into the man's eyes and nose and Gaines cried out and finally brought his hands up to tear away those punishing fingers.

Miles wrenched free and swung savagely, his breath coming in ragged gusts. He sank his left deep into Gaines' stomach and clubbed him with his right as the other sagged. Gaines fell back across the overturned table, his weight collapsing it like matchboard, and Miles fell on top of him, still clubbing with his injured hand, his pain making him half crazy, his rage beyond control.

His foreman and Charlie pulled him off Gaines' prostrate figure. Charlie, a mountain of a man with a bull voice, was growling: 'He's had enough, blast it—'

Miles' dark face turned to the bar owner; his eyes were wild. 'Take your hands off me, Charlie!'

Charlie said: 'Sure, Miles. But take it easy—'

'Take them off!'

Charlie shrugged. He let Miles go, and Cud came back between Miles and Gaines' companions. 'He's had enough,' he said sourly. 'Let's go.'

Miles stood spraddle-legged, shaking hair from his eyes. His efforts at self-control were plainly visible, and the rage in this man held the others in that room unmoving.

His wild gaze picked out Gaines' friends, one by one, and each man evaded that naked challenge. Slowly then Miles wiped the thin line of blood from his chin and bent to find his hat.

Cud took advantage of this to hand out advice to those shaken men. 'Tell Gaines his stuff's been scattered west of the Potholes. Next time he runs them on the Strip we'll leave them for the buzzards!'

Miles turned to Charlie. He was still breathing heavily, but his voice was even. 'Sorry for this mess, Charlie. I'll pay for what's broken. Send me a bill in the morning.'

He turned and walked out, not waiting for his foreman. He bumped into the first of three men just pushing through the batwings, jostled him aside, and went out, not looking back.

Cud Walker, following, paused to let the three men step inside. The man Miles had jostled was about his age; but he looked older. He was taller than Cud, slender and almost painfully neat in town clothes. But he was no town man; there was about his lean, sallow face a harsh and predatory look that caught a man's attention and made for a second wondering glance.

Cud knew him vaguely as Wyeth Brand, a newcomer to the valley. He ran a horse spread in the hills behind Hammer, but spent most of his time in town—kept a room in the hotel

12

which seemed to serve as headquarters for his affairs.

The two men with Brand fell into a familiar pattern to the Hammer foreman. They were lean, hard-faced riders whose guns, worn low and thonged down, were immediately indicative of their occupation.

Cud felt a warning trickle coldly down his spine; he felt the weight of Brand's eyes, a cruel and slitted yellow, as they made their appraisal of him. The abrupt dismissal was almost an insult.

He pushed past them, vaguely disturbed, and slammed the batwings on his way out.

The three men came into the small bar and surveyed the group around Gaines unconscious figure.

Mike O'Lean straightened, his voice bitter in the stillness. 'To blazes with Hammer! I'm stringing along with Ben. We've been kept off the Strip long enough. I for one am going to start moving in!'

Wyeth Brand smiled thinly as he turned to the bar . . .

*　　　　　*　　　　　*

Outside, Miles stopped at the corner and took a deep breath. His anger was still raw and violent and he felt the physical need of an outlet. He looked down the night-darkened street, past the straggle of dingy buildings that here and there glowed with yellow lamplight. Across the dark sweep of country the hills made a ragged barrier against the low-hanging stars.

Six months ago his father had ridden toward those hills—and disappeared, as casually and completely as though Farnum North had never existed.

Nor did the short, simply worded note his father had mailed to him in Chicago make sense to Miles.

It read:

'It's been almost twenty years since I've gone through Saddle Pass to the Dune country. Something's come up—I've got to go back. I'm telling no one, not even your mother. Come home and take over Hammer. Don't try to come after me. I made a bad mistake once—if I can straighten it out I'll be back. If not, good luck, son . . .'

Cud's troubled voice came, intruding into his thoughts. 'I'll bring the hosses around, Miles.' And he stepped off into the darkness as the boss of Hammer nodded impatiently.

Miles fumbled in his shirt pocket for his Bull Durham. His right hand was throbbing and his fingers felt like sausages as he tried to roll himself a smoke. He spilled most of the tobacco and finally gave it up as a bad job.

He waited for Cud, staring moodily down the shadowed street. Chuckline. A one-horse town set in the middle of nowhere—a

14

crossroads settlement that had little hope of ever getting bigger or more important than it was right now.

He tried to pin down his dislike.

Farnum North had been too restless, stung by too quick an ambition, to spend much time with his wife after his marriage. Gail North, youngest daughter of an impoverished southern planter, had married Farnum in the belief he would again give her the comforts and standing she had enjoyed as a girl. She had followed him from Virginia to St. Louis, where she had remained to give birth to Miles.

She had waited here, grubbing out a dingy existence in grimy rooms on Water Street; waited for Farnum's infrequent letters. If she began to lose hope, it had not been apparent to young Miles. But her beauty had faded quickly, and stubbornness had pinched her face and bowed her shoulders.

And finally a letter had come from Farnum; he had struck it rich. They were to join him at Chuckline, a town she had never heard of, in West Texas, beyond the wild Pecos River.

Hammer was a few shacks and a comfortable three-room house when they arrived. The additions were due to Gail's planning. It seemed, in those first years, as if Farnum were determined to make up to his wife for the long years he had failed her. Miles remembered them as the happiest years of his life.

They had had no other children. Gail had given birth to two stillborn offspring and then Doctor Kedner had advised her not to have any more . . .

Miles had grown up in this country—he knew the land from the craggy Diamonds to the canyon-slashed badlands west of the river as well as he knew the back of his hand.

It was a long way from Chicago—a longer way from the dreams he had taken with him to medical school. In West Texas Hammer meant something—in Chicago it meant nothing.

In Chicago he had found a world apart from Hammer—something of the world his mother had dreamed of and finally gave up hoping for; a world of nuances and values that had no counterpart in Chuckline . . .

Just a country boy with the smell of hay still in my hair, he thought, and the remembrance stirred all the old bitterness which he had never completely laid away to rest.

While living the small but intimate social life of a medical student he had met a girl and fallen in love. She was the daughter of one of the school's business administrators—her name was Lucille Ward. A popular girl, gay and charming—she had seemed to enjoy his company.

But he would always remember that his father's letter, calling him back to Hammer, had come a day too late; twenty-four hours too late to save him from Lucille's icily polite refusal.

'But, Miles dear, you didn't really think I—'

He had come back to Hammer, his ego shaken, his belief in himself dimmed. He had met Kate Barrow, who had come from the same world as Lucille Ward, and he had sought her out, finding in her acceptance of him a solace for the wound in his soul.

Now as he waited for his foreman, he had the recurring troubling thought that he was not being fair to Kate—

Cud came up then, riding his bay and leading a big-chested roan horse. Miles shook his head in sudden decision. 'I'll walk. Meet me at Doc Kcdner's. I'm going to have this hand looked after.'

Cud nodded. He hesitated a moment. 'It ain't gonna end with what happened tonight, Miles,' he said.

Miles shrugged.

'Mike O'Lean and the boys with Gaines were yore friends once,' Cud muttered. 'They never gave Hammer any trouble—'

Miles scowled. 'What did you expect me to do, Cud? Let them walk in and take over the Strip? Heck, you know how things were when I got back. You pointed it out to me yourself. We were being crowded by every two-bit nester in the Basin.'

The Hammer foreman looked thoughtful. 'Yore father was letting things slide,' he admitted. 'Something was bothering him,

17

something that seemed to take all interest from him. I caught him several times staring toward Saddle Pass.' Cud shrugged. 'Happened right after he got the letter I told you about. I just saw the envelope—whatever was inside he kept to himself. But he seemed to go soft then—'

Miles' face was stiff in the shadows. 'You don't get anywhere being soft, Cud,' he said grimly. Then, abruptly: 'See you outside Kedner's!'

Cud looked after the big man and shook his head.

CHAPTER THREE

Miles walked down the street, feeling the letdown take the spring from his stride. He had come to town keyed up and angry—what had happened in Charlie's hadn't really settled anything. He had the unsettling feeling that Gaines was only a pawn in a bigger game directed at Hammer—a tool to be used to turn Hammer's old friends against him.

From the beginning, from the day he had returned to Hammer, Miles had run into a disturbing feeling of mystery. In all the years he had lived here he had been given no inkling of anything in his father's life which would lead Farnum to do what he had done.

Disregarding the warning in his father's letter, he had ridden through Saddle Pass to the arid bleakness of the Dune country, where ceaseless winds off the scarred buttes moved and rearranged in endless patterns the hills of sand that ran like momentarily frozen waves to the far bulk of the black-lava ridges.

He had found nothing to explain why his father had come this way—or what he had wanted here.

But from that day little things had begun to trouble Hammer. Stock stolen. Waterholes made undrinkable. Riders shot at. No one had been killed; only one man had been wounded, and the wound was just a shallow gash across his upper arm. Whoever was doing the sniping was staying at long range; unless he was an exceedingly bad shot he did not seem interested in hitting his target. But the net result of this war of nerves had been that Hammer had lost four riders and a grim tension had built up among the other hands.

And then there was this Gaines thing. The waterholes on the Strip provided most of the water, during dry spells, for Hammer beef. In his father's time, the few nester-farmers bordering the Strip had been allowed to water their stock there. But they had worked with Farnum on this, not tried to take over. Since Gaines arrival, the man seemed bent on deliberately stirring up trouble for Hammer . . .

Three men, talking in low tones in front of the General Store, became silent as he passed, and Miles smiled thinly. The wind was hot off the arid land to the south—hot and irritating. It rustled through Chuckline like some bad-tempered animal, nosing down alleys, whining its dislike.

Miles was tired. He felt his shoulders sag as he paused before Doc Kedner's place. Kedner lived over Tanner's Harness Shop. Miles went up the long flight of outside stairs and knocked on the door with the small, neatly lettered sign: HARRY M. KEDNER, M.D.

A girl came and opened the door for him. He said tiredly: 'Your dad in, Cobina?'

The girl stood almost eye level with him. A tall, slim-bodied woman, nevertheless she did not give the impression of frailty. Her hair was knotted in a bun on her neck; it was a rich brown illuminated by the soft light behind her.

He had known Cobina for fifteen years and he took her presence here as casually as he took the dark leather chairs, the ugly settee, the dark walnut-stained bookcase with its set of medical books in sober bindings.

Miles had grown up with Cobina Kedner, attended the Basin school with her, had fished in Cottonwood Creek with her. He had taken this girl's companionship as naturally as he had taken growing up—and then he had gone off to Chicago, to medical school, and when he had returned she was a woman and everything had changed.

She said: 'Yes, he's in the parlor, reading his journal.' She closed the door as he stepped inside and looked quickly at his swelling right hand, then up into his face.

'When?'

He lifted his shoulders. 'Fifteen minutes ago.' He walked past her to sink his big frame into a chair, and she looked after him a moment, her eyes soft, womanly. She had a pert face which was sensitive and intelligent as well, but her cheeks dimpled when she smiled and her eyes took on a glow that transformed the pertness to beauty.

'I'll go fetch him, Miles,' she said, and went across the small, comfortable office to the living quarters in the rear.

A few moments later a thick-bodied man with muttonchop graying whiskers and wearing gold-framed spectacles came into the room.

He said: 'Hello, Miles.' He glanced at Miles' hand and whistled tunelessly. 'Again,' he murmured, and pulled up a chair. He took the hand in his and probed with his fingers, ignoring Miles' wince.

'Couple of small bones broken,' he diagnosed readily. He looked up then, pushing his spectacles up on his high forehead. 'I warned you before, son—your hands are too brittle for the use you give them. Allow them time to heal this time.'

Miles grunted. He waited stoically as the

21

doctor bandaged his hand. Cobina remained in the rear doorway. Kedner finished his job and settled back. 'Keep your arm in a sling for a few days,' he advised. Then, 'Who was it this time?'

Miles got up and reached for his hat. 'Ben Gaines,' he answered shortly. He pulled the injured fingers of his hand into a fist, grimaced, and slowly straightened them out. 'How much Doc?'

Kedner shrugged. 'I'll bill you.'

He got up and faced Miles, shorter than the younger man by almost a foot.

'Why did you do it?' he asked.

Miles frowned. 'Gaines?'

Kedner nodded. 'He took over Canady's place, didn't he?'

Miles' lips curled. 'That ain't all he wants to take over, Harry. And he seems to have talked the rest of the boys along the Strip into siding with him—'

'The others were your father's friends,' Kedner pointed out. 'Have you tried talking to them?'

Miles wheeled and headed for the door. Then he stopped and looked back at the doctor. His voice was hard. 'Harry, I came to get my hand fixed, not to listen to a sermon!'

'Maybe it's time someone gave you a sermon!' Kedner snapped. He stood in the middle of the room, a stubborn scowl on his broad face.

Once this man had been his protégé. It had been at his advice that Miles had gone to medical school. A widower, with an only child, a daughter, he had allowed himself to build on the future . . .

'Your father was everyone's friend in the Basin. Hammer was a brand which had helped build up everything worthwhile here. Since your return you've seemed set to smash everything your father built up here!'

Miles stared at the angry, bull-necked doctor, a stoniness masking his thoughts. He understood the rancor behind the man's speech, yet it hurt—and he felt a sense of futility that kept him from trying to explain Hammer's troubles to this man. Kedner knew only the surface of what was happening in the Basin—

So he said flatly: 'If it has to be that way, Doc, I will. I'll smash Gaines if he tries to move in on Hammer—and I'll break O'Lean and Shorty and the others if they back Gaines!'

Kedner took a deep breath. He came across the room to Miles, harshness pinching his mouth. 'Miles! I remember when you wanted to be a doctor, like me. It made me proud. What happened? What happened in Chicago to change you?'

Miles' eyes went a flinty gray. 'Maybe it's because I found out money is what counts, Harry. Money and the power it gives you!'

Doctor Kedner stared at that grim face,

sensing the bitterness behind it, wondering what flame had tempered the man inside.

He said wearily: 'Being a country doctor is the hard way, eh? Too slow?'

Miles' lips twisted sourly. 'Too slow,' he nodded, and went out, closing the door behind him.

Kedner stood staring. From across the room Cobina said quietly: 'Your coffee's getting cold, Dad.' He turned and looked sharply at her before crossing the office.

*   *   *

Miles came down the stairs and paused on the edge of the walk, waiting for Cud. A flattened, reddish moon stained the sky. It had been that kind of moon that had been in the sky when he had left Chuckline two years ago.

He felt the weight of his Colt against his hip, and he brought his left hand up and looked at it. From the classroom of Doctor Leyton remembered words echoed in his head: 'A good surgeon's hand must be quick, sure and confident. A miscalculation of a fraction of an inch when performing an abdominal operation may mean death for the patient.'

A world remote from Chuckline—from Doctor Kedner. Kedner was a good country doctor, but he knew little of the latest medical discoveries. He still prescribed calomel and sulphur; he had patients who believed in

24

wearing evil-smelling herbs in a cloth sack suspended around their necks to ward off the evil spirits of sickness.

Kedner was right. He had wanted to be a doctor more than anything else. Then he had met Lucille Ward and discovered that money and good manners meant more to her than medical ambitions and ideals; because he had been in love with her his own values had been shaken. He had come back to Hammer because of his father's letter; but he had come back determined to make Hammer a power in the State of Texas. Way down and tied to the hurt inside him was a desire to make Hammer big enough to come to the attention of Lucille Ward . . .

A sudden revulsion shook him. He turned and headed down the walk, not waiting for his foreman. The lights of Slade's Bar fell across his path, and he turned and went inside.

Midweek business was slow. Three men stood by the bar—they didn't look around until Miles joined them.

Ned Atwell was talking to a lanky, serious-faced farmer from the Teneras bottoms.

' . . . get a combine together . . . sell stock. Irrigation would change the picture for you boys down there. It's the only answer to drought—'

He turned as Miles came up. Hammer's boss grinned sourly. 'Still hammering at your pet project, Ned?'

Ned's face was flushed. He had been drinking more than he usually did and his tongue was a little thick. 'Some day the small fellows around here will get sense, Miles. They'll get together and tap the Cottonwood and bring water down to the bottoms.'

Miles said evenly: 'From the Cottonwood to Morris' place is Hammer grass. Or have you forgotten?'

Morris shoved his partially empty beer glass aside, grinned meagerly, and moved away. 'Wife's waiting for me, Ned—'

The young lawyer nodded. He turned to Miles. They had formed a ready friendship soon after Miles' return from Chicago. But then Kate Barrow had come between them— she stood between them now and he couldn't dismiss her.

Yet he lacked the courage to tell Miles. In many ways he was like Kate. He sensed the violence in this big man and always, when he tried to let Miles know about him and Kate, his courage deserted him.

He shrugged now, bending his eyes away from Miles' gaze. 'Some day you'll see I'm right, Miles. For Hammer as well as for the smaller ranchers here—'

North put a hand on Ned's shoulder. 'Forget it, Ned. I have enough troubles without you adding to them, too. Here, let me buy you a drink—'

Atwell pulled away. 'Some other time,

Miles. I guess I've had enough for tonight.'

Miles watched him turn and walk stiffly toward the doors.

CHAPTER FOUR

Sheriff Carl Masters came out of the lunchroom, and paused a moment on the boardwalk while he ruminatively rolled his toothpick to the other side of his mouth. Chuckline was quiet—even more quiet than usual for a middle-of-the-week night. Yet he felt a vague uneasiness, a premonition of trouble that pressed disturbingly down on him.

He crossed the light-splotched street and walked to the corner, turning left to the law office. It was a long oblong of adobe, with his office and two cells facing the street, living quarters in the rear.

'Baldy' Simms, his deputy, was playing solitaire at the big desk. The oil lamp at his elbow highlighted his seamed, tobacco-stained face, lending to him years which were not there. Baldy was a short, spare-fleshed man in his late twenties, yet he looked older than Masters, who was crowding the middle thirties.

Masters was a tall man, strongly built, with a square, ruddy face cast in genial lines. But often there crept into his blue eyes a bleak and far-away look that stripped the pleasantness from him, revealing the bedrock of uncompromising hardness.

Masters was a widower. He had lost his wife and two small children in a typhus epidemic, all within three months of one another. He had been a widower for eight years now.

Baldy was a drifter. He had been orphaned young enough not to remember his folks, only an uncle who had seven other children and hadn't had time to pay much attention to his nephew.

Simms had worked at a dozen occupations in his restless life, from track layer to dishwasher and cowhand. He seemed to have settled for his present job. Much of the reason for this lay with Masters; in the older man Baldy had found the steadiness and understanding he might have found in his father.

They made a good team, and in the years they had been in the Basin, the law had been well handled.

Masters dropped his hat on a chair and, unbuckling his heavy cartridge belt, hung it up on the hook above it. He reached around Baldy and pulled out a desk drawer and found his pipe and a tin of tobacco.

His deputy flipped his last card over, scowled over his layout. His voice noncommittal.

'No trouble?'

Masters tamped down tobacco into his

28

thick-crusted briar 'Heard Miles was in town with his foreman,' he said 'Might be trouble.' He lighted up, his eyes moody and withdrawn shining flatly in the reddish flare of his match.

'Something's riding the boy.' Baldy nodded 'Can't say as I blame him, either, Carl—'

Masters shrugged. He had not known young North too well, nor for that matter, had he been too familiar with old Farnum North. He had been more than surprised when Farnum had stopped by the office, the day before he left the valley and handed him a thick sealed envelope

'Keep this for me, Carl?' he had asked. There had been nothing in Farnum's bluff face, in his tone, to indicate that he would never come back.

The sheriff had hefted the envelope, nodded. 'Sure. What is it—your will?'

Farnum's face had shown a quick smile. 'Might be,' he had said casually 'I'll be around later in the week for it. But—' he had hesitated only a fleeting moment; his eyes had held a worried glint—'just in case I don't come back for it, keep it for me, for my boy. Miles. He'll be coming back from medical school.'

'Sure,' Masters had said. 'I'll put it in the safe with my fifty dollars. I don't trust the bank, either.' And he remembered now that the joke had seemed to make no impression on Farnum.

'Major Barrow is a mite too curious,'

Hammer's boss had replied, frowning. 'I got nothing against the bank, mind you,' he'd amended. 'I keep my money there.' He had hesitated again, then squared his shoulders as though throwing off a weight.

'In case I don't come back, keep this for me for six months. It's important that you do this, Carl. Don't mention having this letter to anyone, not even Baldy. Don't mention it to my wife, nor to Miles. But if I'm not back in six months, open it. Read it. Let Miles know about it then.'

The sheriff had frowned, wondering at the strange urgency in North 'Why what's the matter? You going on a trip?'

Farnum nodded 'A trip I knew I would have to take some day, Carl'

They had gone out to the Green Front Saloon and had a drink together and talked about cows and Miles and doctoring, and then Farnum had ridden off. Masters had not seen him again, even though, with Miles, he had ridden through Saddle Pass to the Dune country and found nothing to indicate why Farnum North had gone there. Nor had subsequent queries to law offices as far north as five hundred miles revealed anyone who had seen a man answering Farnum's description.

Carl still had the sealed envelope in his safe; it was typical of him that, though he had his normal share of curiosity, he had obeyed

30

Farnum's wishes. It lacked a week of six months since Farnum had left that letter with him; he remembered it clearly now.

He remembered it all the more sharply because of the changes that had come to the Basin since Farnum had ridden away. The peace and quiet were gone now. With Canaday's death a small link in the outfits bordering Hammer had been broken and filled by Benjamin Gaines, a newcomer to the Basin. And with Gaines' coming had started the discord which seemed to be affecting the entire Diamonds country.

The sheriff sighed slightly and turned to the window to look out on the dark street. The lamplight was shining against the dirty panes, reflecting his tall figure; he saw Baldy watching him.

'We've had it easy too long, Baldy.' he muttered. 'For the past six months it's been building—a pattern of trouble I can't figger. And Farnum's boy is like a match—he can be scraped into fire!'

Baldy shuffled his cards. 'New riders in town every day,' he said. He was thinking aloud, weighing the trouble he and the sheriff sensed building. 'I don't like that horse outfit, Carl, nor the man who runs it—Wyeth Brand. He don't fit easy in town clothes, to my way of thinking. And if those gun-hung riders he has with him are bronc busters, then the breed shore has changed!'

31

Masters made no comment. His thoughts moved back to Miles. He had known the man only from occasional meetings before young North had gone off to medical school, but he had picked up a lot from small talk in town and from Hammer riders.

The kid had been set on being a doctor. He was Doc Kedner's protégé, and Harry had been proud of him. And the sheriff had not been too hard-crusted to sense what Doc Kedner's daughter thought of Miles.

Then Miles had come back to the Basin, and he had come back hard. At first Masters had taken the change in the man to be the result of his father's strange disappearance.

But Miles' utter silence concerning his medical career, his courtship of the Barrow girl, his grim temper, were out of character with what he had known of the boy. Something had hurt Miles while he had been away—

The sound of a man walking quickly toward the office intruded into the sheriff's thoughts. He felt trouble in the quick steps, and behind him Baldy laid his cards aside and came to his feet.

Mike O'Lean burst into the office and swung around to face the sheriff. His thin, bitter face had the hard shine of excitement and anger.

'There's been trouble over at Charlie's!' he snapped. 'Miles North and his foreman, Walker. Miles beat the stuffing out of

Gaines—broke his jaw, I think.'

The sheriff took in Mike's belligerent attitude. 'Who caused the trouble?'

'Miles!' O'Lean's voice was harsh. 'Walked in on the bunch of us in Charlie's an' picked a fight with Ben. Told him to keep his cows off the Strip—told all of us to keep our beef off Strip grass an' water—'

'It's Hammer's water,' Baldy cut in mildly. 'Miles has a right to keep Ben's cows off the Strip.'

'The devil it is!' O'Lean snapped angrily. 'I thought so, too. So did the rest of the boys. But Ben says it ain't so. Miles don't own the waterholes on the Strip.'

Baldy's mouth hardened. 'If Ben told you that he's a liar. I checked the records over at the land office myself. Farnum North owns the Strip legal—'

Mike whirled on him. 'You working for Hammer, Baldy?' he snapped.

Baldy reddened. 'I'm trying to point out some facts to you, Mike,' he said stubbornly, 'something you seem to be over-looking these days—'

Masters cut in coldly. 'Let's stick to what happened tonight. I'll come over and have a talk with Ben and Miles—'

'Miles left,' Mike growled.

'I'll find him,' the sheriff stated. He reached for his hat and gunbelt. His deputy turned for his headgear, and Carl said: 'No need for both

33

of us, Baldy. I'll be back shortly.'

Baldy stood by the desk and watched Masters go out, O'Lean at his heels. He did not like the eagerness in the little man, nor the quick beat of excitement in his voice.

There was trouble pushing Mike, coming to a head . . .

*   *   *

Doctor Kedner was in Charlie's Bar, finishing with Ben Gaines, when Sheriff Masters walked in. Gaines was slumped in a chair. He had a hurt, sullen look about him. His jaw was bandaged, as though he had a bad toothache.

The sheriff guessed Ben would be sipping soup a long time.

He asked a few questions to which Gaines mumbled sullen answers. Mike answered for him. The way O'Lean stated it, Miles had come in looking for trouble, had provoked Ben into a fight . . .

The sheriff's glance drifted to the three men at the bar. Wyeth Brand and his two riders seemed only casually interested in what had happened; yet it occurred to Masters that this trouble had begun shortly after Brand had come into the Basin.

Doc Kedner pushed his roll of bandages into his bag and snapped it shut. He stood up and turned to the sheriff, a scowl on his whiskered face. 'Can't understand the boy,

34

Carl,' he snapped. 'He's been walking around with a chip on his shoulder since he came back. He used to be a good-natured boy—'

'Might be he has something to get riled about,' Masters interrupted dryly.

Harry Kedner shrugged. He picked up his bag and turned away, and the sheriff faced the man in the chair. Mike O'Lean stood by Ben like a bantam rooster, head cocked belligerently to one side.

'If you've been ranging your beef on Hammer grass, Gaines,' the sheriff said mildly, 'then you've been asking for trouble. That goes for all of you,' he added.

Mike stiffened. 'You backing Hammer in this, Carl?'

'I'm backing whoever's right,' Masters said inflexibly. 'Heck, Mike, I know the fix you're in; the same fix most of the small Basin ranchers are in. The boys down in the Teneras bottoms are in no better shape. If this drought continues you stand to lose what little stock you have—'

'Not as long as there's water on the Strip, I won't!' Mike snapped angrily. 'Old Farnum North always let me water my stock at the springs. I'm going to keep watering there!'

Masters shook his head. 'Then why do it the hard way, Mike? What's gotten into you fellows? None of you would have forced your way onto the Strip if Farnum was alive. Why push Miles?'

'I'll push the dirty son!' Gaines' voice was a whisper; it hurt him to force the words between his swollen lips. 'I'm not afraid of Hammer!'

Masters' blue eyes lost their kindliness. 'Not as long as I'm sheriff you won't, Ben!' he said curtly. 'Maybe it's time I warned you—all of you. I don't want a range war in the Basin. I'll arrest the first man who steps out of line, from tonight on. That goes for you small ranchers on the other side of Dogbone—and for Hammer!'

Gaines sneered. Mike's eyes held open rebellion. Shorty Baker and Dutch Muehler shrugged. Joe Larsen said quietly: 'I'm not tangling with Hammer, Carl.'

The sheriff nodded. 'If it's not too late, maybe you can talk to Miles. But remember this: the Strip belongs to Hammer. If you want water you'll have to make a deal with Miles— or find some other way. But not your way, Ben—not your way at all!'

He turned on his heel and left them then. Behind him the bar was quiet.

Gaines' eyes lifted to Brand at the bar, and a quick look passed between them. Brand was smiling faintly as he turned to the drink in his hand.

The sheriff paused on the corner and stared down the dark street. He felt the hot wind in his face—it stirred the uneasy temper in him. The low-hanging stars blazed in a velvet

36

setting—the moon was going down, staining the western hills with its orange glow.

Trouble was building fast; he knew it now and knew, too, he could do little to stem it. Mike O'Lean was stringing along with Gaines, and he would drag the others with him.

He'd have to have a talk with Miles. Maybe he'd better open Farnum's letter—he had the sudden feeling that it would explain a lot that had happened since the elder North had disappeared.

Still, he had promised Farnum to wait six months—the boss of Hammer had been strangely adamant on this point. And it still lacked a week—

He sighed heavily and turned toward the office. He'd ride out and have a talk with Miles in the morning—and then he'd have a look at Brand's horse spread. He was getting curious about this newcomer . . .

He saw Hammer's foreman, Cud Walker, come out of the shadows, riding his horse and leading Miles' big black. Cud pulled up at Slade's Bar and went inside, and the sheriff moved quickly, turning to the batwings only a few paces behind the man.

Miles was alone at the bar; he had evidently been drinking. His right hand was bandaged and in a sling. There was a dark flush on his face, an edgy glitter in his smoky gray eyes.

Walker was beside him, a worried look on his face. He was waiting for Miles to finish his

37

drink.

Miles turned around as the sheriff came up; he nodded shortly. 'Figured you'd be in, Carl,' he said. His tone was slightly belligerent.

Masters said: 'I saw Gaines. I'm giving you the same advice I gave him and the others. There's going to be no range war in the Basin while I'm sheriff!'

Miles' grin was crooked. 'I've closed the Strip, Carl,' he said thickly. 'If that means war, it'll have to be war! I'm through being pushed around!'

'It's a bad time for pushing—all the way around,' Carl agreed. His voice had a kindly note. 'The Strip belongs to Hammer—closing its water off is your right. But for the sake of peace in the Basin, share it. I'll pay off in the long run, son. Your father knew that—'

'I'm running Hammer!' Miles reminded him. 'And starting next week I'm running a thousand head of Hammer beef onto the Strip. I'm going to need that water for my stock—I'm not going to stand by and be crowded off my own range by Ben Gaines and the fools he's talked into backing him!'

Masters sighed. 'You're within your rights,' he repeated, 'if you want it that way. But remember, Miles—I'm the law. The first time you try to enforce your stand with a gun, against Gaines or the others, I'm coming after you. I told Gaines the same thing!'

Miles watched the sheriff walk out. Masters

meant what he said: Miles knew it. But he had a feeling that Masters wouldn't be able to check the trouble aimed at Hammer—that only Hammer's guns could do it.

Walker's voice was sour. 'Let's ride, Miles . . .'

The moon was long gone from the sky—the town lay quiet under the stars.

A dark shape detached itself from the inky blackness of the building shadows and crossed the empty, weedy lot to the back of the law office.

The window facing the lot was dark. A cat came prowling around the corner and stiffened at the thin, tall shadow which whirled . . . A gun glinted in reflected starlight and the figure cursed softly.

The cat jumped sidewise and faded into the blackness.

The prowler waited a moment. He was a sinewy, long-necked man. He raised his left fist and pounded on the sheriff's back door.

There was a creaking of bedsprings inside. 'What in tarnation's up?' The sheriff's sleepy voice held irritation.

The man waiting outside said sharply: 'Trouble, Sheriff! Hurry!'

Masters stumbled around in the dark. From across the room Baldy cursed. A match scraped, and the small flame wavered and then grew into a yellow glare as the deputy found the lamp near his bunk.

The sheriff was pulling on his pants. He bent to put on his boots as Baldy, clad in longjohns, sleepily scratched his bald pate.

'Some darned fool—' the sheriff mumbled, reaching for his cartridge belt. He turned to the door, pulled it open. 'Where's the trouble—?'

The Colt jammed against his stomach made a muffled, heavy sound. The explosion seemed to push Masters back into the room; he tottered, his eyes bulging, and the gun blasted again. Carl clutched at his middle; he tried to step away from the door, and then his legs went rubbery and he fell.

Baldy was still blinded by the lamplight. He turned to face the door, and the heavy slug caught him in the chest and flung him back against the table like a rag doll. His arm swept the lamp off the rickety table. It smashed on the floor, and in the sudden darkness the killer flung one more shot at Baldy's tottering figure before he turned and ran for the shadows on the far side of the empty lot . . .

CHAPTER FIVE

The shooting shocked Chuckline. For years gun trouble had bypassed the Basin. It was generally agreed that Carl Masters and his deputy, Baldy, had been in good measure responsible for the years of comparative peace.

Now Masters was dead. Baldy was still alive—but Doctor Kedner gave him only a fifty-fifty chance to pull through.

Overnight the Basin found itself without law enforcement at a time when the ugly threat of range war brewed over the dry, brittle-tempered land.

Major John Barrow, accepted pillar of Chuckline society and one of its most influential citizens, was considering this abrupt loss in his wood-paneled office in the Basin Bank when Miss Emily Tinsey, spinster bookkeeper and secretary, entered to announce a caller.

'A Mr. Brand,' she said. Miss Tinsey had an alum-puckered mouth and disapproving eyes. 'He says he knows you, Major.'

Major Barrow frowned introspectively. He was a tall, erect man with an air of great dignity enhanced by graying temples. His black mustache was cropped close and neat in military style, and his features were smooth and firm despite his fifty years. He had a sharp, incisive way of speaking which was attributed to his years in the Army. When he had come to Chuckline he had let it be known that he was recently retired, and few people bothered to speculate why Major Barrow had chosen Chuckline as a place for retirement, or why he was retired at an age when most Army officers were still bucking for promotion.

41

He sat behind his walnut desk, turning the name Brand over in his mind, trying to place the name in his past. He nodded briefly to the waiting secretary. 'Yes—show him in.'

He remembered having seen the man in town. Wasn't he the owner of a horse spread in the Diamonds?

Wyeth Brand entered the office behind Miss Tinsey. He was quietly dressed, but even so Major Barrow's eyes narrowed abruptly. This man was no ordinary business man. The Major had been around men of violence too long not to smell the signs—there was a predatory, feline grace in this man, a harsh cruelty in his tightened mouth. He was not wearing a gun, but Wyeth Brand was none the less dangerous because of this . . .

The caller waited patiently until Miss Tinsey had retreated, closing the office door behind her.

'Sit down, Mr. Brand,' Major Barrow said. He waved a friendly hand to a chair. 'What can I do for you?'

Brand's face held a quiet, controlled contempt. He did not sit down. He came to the edge of the desk, facing the banker.

'More than you are thinking, Major,' he said.

Barrow straightened in his chair, his features losing their professional friendliness. His eyes had a frowning, wary regard.

'Are you threatening me, sir?'

Brand reached for the cigar box on Barrow's desk and took one without invitation. 'You and me met before,' he said ungrammatically. 'Only you don't remember—and I haven't forgotten.'

Major Barrow licked his lips. 'Were you in the Army, Mr. Brand?'

'I managed to avoid that unprofitable line of business,' Brand said. His tone held little humor. 'But I happened to be in Westfield when they drummed a certain major out of the Army. For malfeasance, I think they called it at the court-martial. A fancy name for a crook, eh? I think they found that major guilty of misappropriating supply funds—'

Barrow's face had turned ashen. He stammered: 'You must be mistaken, Mr. Brand. I don't know whom you are referring to—'

'Perhaps you'd like to have the mayor check with Army authorities,' Brand suggested thinly.

Barrow seemed to collapse in his chair. All his dignity was gone; lines ran deep down the sides of his pinched mouth.

He said heavily, 'I've come a long way to bury myself in a small town, to live that day down. I've got a daughter who was away at school at the time. She doesn't know—'

'I didn't come in here to expose you,' Brand interrupted harshly. He bit off a small end of the cigar, spat it out on the floor and lighted up. 'You go along with me and I promise you no one will ever know. You might even make money out of it.' Brand's smile was feline and mirthless. 'Money does interest you, doesn't it Major?'

Barrow rose. He walked hurriedly to the door, pulled it open a few inches and peered out. He glimpsed Miss Tinsey working at her desk and closed it gently.

He turned back to the desk, wiping his brow with a clean white handkerchief. 'She's got a long nose and a sharp ear,' he muttered in explanation of his actions.

Brand shrugged.

Barrow faced him across the desk. He looked smaller somehow, with his shoulders slumped, his face tired, his eyes desperate.

'What do you want of me?'

'You're the head of the county commissioners,' Brand replied. 'With Masters dead, and his deputy laid up, a new sheriff will have to be appointed.' He lifted up a hand to halt Major Barrow's forming protest. 'I don't give a hang how you do it, Major. But your job will be to talk the other members into appointing the man I name. Maybe the two men I have in mind—we'll be needing a deputy, too.'

Barrow wagged his head. 'I don't know—I don't know—'

'You'd better know!' Brand snapped relentlessly. 'You go along with this, or I'll let the whole town know what kind of man is running the Basin Bank—'

Barrow slumped back in his chair. 'I'll do my best. Who—what's the name of the new sheriff?'

'Red Shaner.' Brand grinned. 'I'll vouch for him. He's a fast hand with a gun—the Basin is going to need him. The deputy is Von Sesta. They both work for me. I'll be loaning them to the county.'

Barrow said thickly: 'I can't force two comparative strangers into office, Brand. I've got to have something more to go by—'

'I'll give it to you,' Brand growled. 'Shaner'll have a letter of recommendation from the United States Marshal's office.'

Barrow wiped his brow again. 'What do you want out of this, Mr. Brand? What are you after?'

Brand's lips curled. His voice was a thin, implacable whisper. 'Hammer!'

Major Barrow remained in his office long after his visitor had departed. He stood staring at the pine-paneled wall in a sort of blind, unfeeling futility.

He had thought he had buried his past here in Chuckline. He had been careful. He had worked his way into the respect of the Basin. Time and again he had felt the prod of ruthless ambition, seeing opportunities to make a killing—and he had buried these feelings down deep.

When Miles had come to court his daughter

45

he had felt that prod of ambition again. Hammer was a big ranch, the biggest in the Basin. John Barrow had immediately seen how he could make it bigger.

Farnum North had been content to consolidate what he had built up—he had spread out so far, and no farther. But Barrow had the feeling that Miles could be prodded into a bigger move for power.

Thinking this, John Barrow had been dreaming lately—seeing himself grow with Hammer; seeing himself as the guiding hand, making Hammer into a far-flung spread, a power in the state.

Now Hammer was lost to him. He closed his eyes, but he could not push aside Brand's thin, cruel features or the amber glitter in his eyes as he had whispered the word, Hammer.

He would have to go along with the man—play the role of puppet instead of master. Anger rose in him and beat hard against the grim facts arrayed against him.

Who was Brand? A newcomer to the Basin. Owner of a horse spread in the Diamonds. Yet what else was he? Perhaps there was an Achilles heel in Brand's past, too. Else why should the man go after Hammer this way?

He stirred then, his jaw tightening harshly. Someone had brutally murdered Sheriff Masters last night, and dangerously wounded his deputy. Who? He had an inkling now who had been behind the killing—but he would never be able to prove it.

A cold sweat started out over him as he considered new possibilities of action. If he acceded to Wyeth Brand's demand the man would control Chuckline—in due time he would control Hammer!

But he knew that he would do as Brand wanted—knew it with a sudden cold, empty feeling which made the room suddenly unbearable. He was in no position to refuse Brand . . .

He rose and took his hat and coat from the hall tree by the door and went out, not even looking around at Miss Tinsey's startled face . . .

*   *   *

It took Major Barrow the better part of the day to convince the other members of the commission to appoint the new sheriff and deputy.

They had met in Mayor Gammison's home, a small group of worried citizens who knew they had a range war brewing on their hands; a war that would affect not only the participants, but all the Basin as well.

John Barrow used all his powers of smooth persuasion to convince these men of the honesty, integrity and need of the two comparative strangers who stood before them. He lied and cajoled them, while Red Shaner, a sinewy, long-necked man with a red steerhorn mustache and insolent green eyes, lounged and drank of the major's best brandy, and Von Sesta, a short, wiry, dark-faced breed, kept picking his teeth with the thin blade of a pocket knife.

In the end he put himself up as a guarantee of the worth of these men—but it was the pressing need of the moment, plus the tangible fact of the forged letter of recommendation, that convinced those men.

They swore Red Shaner in as sheriff that evening and hired Von Sesta as his deputy. They gave Shaner the keys to the law office and mentally prayed they were doing right.

Red Shaner rubbed his sinewy, powerful hands down over the butts of his bone-handled Colts as Barrow pinned Masters' star to his vest. He raised his right hand and repeated the oath in clipped, unaccented monosyllables.

Von Sesta grinned throughout the ceremony. After the badge was pinned to his vest he rubbed it with his sleeve and grinned wider. He seemed to take it as a bright joke.

Wyeth Brand was waiting in the Green Front saloon when they entered. He was on his second drink when the new sheriff and his deputy joined him.

The second part of his plan had gone through without a hitch.

The three of them drank together.

48

CHAPTER SIX

The buildings of Hammer lay in a swale of ground at the western corner of the Basin. It was a big, sprawling ranch watered by two deep-sunk wells pumped by windmills. The Cottonwood came out of the Diamond foothills and crossed Hammer range less than seven miles away before plunging through rocky gorges to lose itself for forty miles through desolate badlands.

Hammer had access to the Cottonwood as well as to the springs on the Strip—drought or no drought, it always had water for its stock. The Cottonwood never ran dry as did the Salt, running south of Dogbone—nor did the springs of the Strip.

Farnum North had chosen well when he had settled in the Basin. He had been here first, and it had been his prerogative. He had early become aware that water would be the key to the Basin and made sure Hammer would have water.

The Cottonwood was too remote from his neighbors to be of practical use to them, but the springs on the Strip had often meant the difference between survival and ruin for the small ranchers south of Dogbone. Farnum North had not been unkind; he had never stocked Hammer even close to what it could

49

graze, and in times like this he had helped the smaller ranchers through.

Miles remembered this as he came out to the wide ranch-house veranda. Behind him the kitchen sounded to the clatter of breakfast dishes being removed by Maria, the Mexican housekeeper. Juan, her husband and a horse wrangler, was busy in the corral, breaking a short-coupled, mean-eyed roan. Nine-year-old Tony, his son, was perched on the top rail, watching his father on the pitching, sun-fishing bronc.

There was an air of peace over the big ranch that had an evanescent quality this morning. It had been too quiet on Hammer since he had returned from Chuckline. In three days there had been no one shot at—no stock reported stolen.

The peace had a brooding quality that held, for Miles, a faint menace. Hammer was too far up the Basin to be of easy access to Chuckline, too far from its nearest neighbors for gossip. It was a little world in itself. Sufficient unto itself for long periods . . .

He stood there, enjoying the early morning coolness—by mid-morning the heat would bear down with brutal hand over the Basin.

He suffered a momentary twinge of conscience as he thought of Kate. He had promised to see her before this—he did not understand his own reluctance. He shook his head and took his hand out of its sling and

50

worked his fingers. The rest had done them a lot of good—the pain was a minor discomfort now as he clenched his fist. He tried rolling himself a smoke and did a passable job of it.

His mother came to the kitchen door and watched him with an anxious expression. There was a tiny hurt in her eyes as she caught the stubborn stance of her son as he stared over the long distances.

She had lost a husband without knowing why—lost him as irrevocably as though she had seen him die. He had ridden away and not come back—and that hurt lay buried deep inside Gail and would never heal, not even if Farnum North were to return today to Hammer.

He had given her no indication that morning—yes, she reminded herself bitterly, in a way he had. Farnum had saddled his bay and then, leaving the horse at the steps, he had come into the kitchen and kissed her gently on the cheek. She had been surprised. His was a gesture not known in the last fifteen years of living together. Farnum North had been a kind husband and a good one, but not a demonstrative one.

Her voice had been sharp (she suffered a twinge of remorse now, remembering). 'Farnum! Have you been drinking?'

He had looked quizzically at her, studying her. She had felt uneasy under his slow regard, and a small voice inside her had whispered: *It's been a long time since there's been any affection in him for you, hasn't it? And do you know why? You killed it, a long time ago—killed it by wanting too much, by asking too much. By forgetting him and wanting only the things you thought important when you were a girl in your father's big house. By remembering bitterly the bad days on Water Street.*

'No, Gail,' he had answered her. 'Not this morning. Not for a long time.' He had turned to go, and she had followed him, her voice softening, a trace of repentance in her. 'Farnum, I'll have dinner waiting. Don't be too long.'

He had looked at her again with a strangely soft, gentle look. 'It's late for that, isn't it?' Then he had touched her arm lightly and smiled and added: 'I'll try to get back for dinner, Gail—' and had gone.

She had not seen him again.

Now she was looking at his son. The hurt inside her grew. Farnum had written to Miles to come home, knowing he would not be coming back from that ride. And Miles had come home. But she did not know her son. The boy who had gone away, the laughing, good-natured boy who had wanted to be a doctor, had returned a hard, taciturn man.

Miles felt her eyes on him and turned; she erased the hurt from her expression before he could notice. She smiled. She still retained a little of her early beauty—she was still slender-

52

waisted, high-bosomed.

She said: 'Is Kate coming out this weekend?'

He shrugged.

She kept her smile, but tiny lines radiated out from her tightening mouth. She liked Kate Barrow. She had things in common with her. But Kate was soft—Kate needed softness in her life, in her man. She would not stand up under trouble. She was the kind who needed to be protected, and the frontier was hard on her kind.

Miles took a deep breath and pushed speculation out of his mind; he moved toward the steps, and now he saw the rider in the distance, small against the rolling hills. He moved down into the yard and waited for him.

Cud Walker pulled his sweated cayuse to a halt by Miles. He sat slack in the saddle, a small man with a tired yet alert face. He said. 'I've got bad news, Miles.'

Miles waited. His mother was still at the door; he could feel her presence. He did not want her to be involved in this, yet he knew he could not keep it from her.

Juan had finished with the bronc—he had climbed to the rail beside his son and was watching Cud with heavy-lidded curiosity as he rolled a smoke with nerve-tired, shaking fingers.

'Ran across Paully, freighting out of Chuckline,' Cud said. 'He had news. Masters is dead. Baldy ain't expected to last through the week.'

Miles took this without visible effect, but the shock rolled through him, sending waves reaching out for hidden meanings.

'When?'

'The night we left town,' Cud replied. He wiped his forehead with his sleeve.

'Who shot them?'

Cud lifted his shoulders. 'Paully didn't know. I gathered no one in town knows. Matt Brecker, up the street from the law office, thought he heard shots sometime after midnight. Didn't think about it, though, until next morning when they found Masters and Baldy. From what Paully said the killer must have awakened them sometime during the night and shot them as they came to the door—'

Miles shifted his gaze to the hills already beginning to blur in the heat haze. The ring was getting tighter around Hammer, he thought; but the pattern eluded him, and the reason.

'You'll be surprised to find there's a new sheriff and deputy in Chuckline,' Cud added thinly. 'A gent named Red Shaner. His deputy is Von Sesta.'

Miles frowned. He couldn't place the men; the names meant nothing to him.

'They worked uncommonly fast,' he muttered. 'Who are they?'

'Nobody knows, rightly,' Cud said dryly.

'Paully said they look as if they have plenty of gun-savvy, though. And it was Major Barrow who talked the mayor and the board of commissioners into appointing them.'

'John Barrow?' Miles' frown deepened. 'John must know them, then—'

'Mebbe,' Cud intruded coldly. 'Mebbe he knows them well enough, Miles. But he's never showed it before. That's why I don't understand it. And what I don't understand I don't like.'

'What do you mean?'

'The way Paully described those gents,' Cud answered, 'I've seen them. Both of them. Once in the hills west of here. The other time in town. They're riders for that horse spread up in the hills. Wyeth Brand's men!'

He let that statement settle in the stillness, his old eyes watching Miles. In the silence that spread between them the clatter of dishes from the house rang sharp and distinct.

'Why?' Miles' voice was a thin urgent whisper. His question had no connection with the conversation; it was an echo of his own surging thoughts. 'Why, Cud?'

Walker understood him, his own thoughts having followed the pattern of Miles' thinking. 'I don't know,' he said. 'If Brand's behind the trouble here, I don't know why.'

The frustration in Miles fretted harshly against growing doubts. He had never been fully convinced that the trouble was generated

55

only by a group of dissatisfied small ranchers south of Dogbone. He had come away from the affair at Charlie's Bar that night with the feeling he had settled nothing by shutting off the Strip's water to them.

True, Gaines had pushed him into a stand against them—a man had his pride, and his was already bruised by what had occurred before his return to the Basin.

But the feeling was strong in him now that Mike O'Lean and the other Dogbone ranchers were only pawns in a bigger move against Hammer—

He said sharply, making his decision on the strength of this, 'I'm riding out to the Strip, Cud. I'm pulling Jack and Lefty away from there—I'm tearing the fence down. I think that's what they wanted all along—' He didn't define the 'they'; he couldn't. That part of the pattern he was not yet sure of.

Cud nodded. 'I'll ride with you.'

Miles shook his head. 'Round up the crew, Cud. Have them waiting for me when I get back. I'll be back by tonight—or tomorrow at the latest. I got a hunch I'll know who we're fighting by then.'

He was saddled and riding in ten minutes. He rode by the house. His mother was still at the door, watching. Walker had gone on into the bunkhouse.

'Don't wait dinner for me,' he said. 'I may not be back—'

He didn't understand the flash of terror which widened her eyes. She made a small gesture of acknowledgement and turned quickly away.

Miles was frowning as he turned the black toward the far lift of the hills.

CHAPTER SEVEN

The Strip was a long narrow valley between two ridges extending like horny fingers from the tumbled, bare-rock Diamonds. Sheltered by these natural barriers, watered by two unfailing springs which Farnum North had turned into small reservoirs, the Strip was the best graze on Hammer.

Beyond the southernmost ridge called Dogbone lay the small spreads of Ben Gaines' Wobbly G, O'Lean's Bar L, Dutch Muehler's Rocking M, Baker's Circle B and Joe Larsen's Lazy L. These were strung out along the Salt bottoms. Larsen's spread, farthest from the Strip, was only eight miles from Chuckline.

Dogbone effectively shut off the Strip from the Salt ranchers, except for a narrow, rock-strewn gulch which splintered it, giving access at the far end to Ben Gaines' spread.

In Farnum's time that narrow passageway had been left open, and Canady, before Gaines, had run his stock onto the Strip this way, whenever the Salt had dried and left him waterless. In those years Farnum had put no barrier across that narrow canyon; but in Farnum's time Hammer had not been threatened from that direction.

Canady and the others had always made their arrangements for water with Hammer beforehand—it had been on a neighborly basis, although Mike O'Lean had sometimes chosen to view it as a 'hat in hand' delegation to Hammer.

Lefty Conners, a rawboned, quiet man in his mid-thirties, had been riding for Hammer for ten years. He had liked working for Farnum, and he liked his job. He had come to the spread at an age when he was inclined to settle down. His was an easy disposition, not prodded by excessive ambition. Perhaps if he had married, he might have found reason to be discontented with his lot. He had his room and board and thirty-five a month. He would never get rich on it.

He had been with Hammer long enough to be confused by the events of the past six months, by the sudden change in the tempo of the spread, the air of violence that had come to break the peace of years.

But he had wedded his loyalties to Hammer; he was staying.

Jack Bevans was a comparative newcomer to Hammer. A slender, boyish-faced man with thinning blond hair and a quicksilver disposition, he was uneasy at Hammer. He needed the job, but he did not have Lefty's deep-seated loyalty; like the older hand, he was confused by the change which had come over the spread with Farnum North's strange disappearance.

In the early morning the smoke from their campfire lifted and bent like a supple gray reed toward Dogbone, rising a scant two hundred yards away.

They had unhitched the wagon and made camp here, using the first day to clear out the jumble of rocks at the canyon mouth and much of the second to dig postholes in the hard, stubborn earth. This morning they had part of the wire up—sundown would see the end of it.

Lefty reached for the coffee pot and poured the black liquid into his cup. His rifle was propped against the wagon wheel fifty feet away.

He kept an eye on the canyon, expecting trouble, if it came, from that direction.

When it did come, it came from another direction—and it came unexpectedly!

They heard horses from the northeast—from the direction of Hammer. Lefty got to his feet and laid his glance on the riders; his brows made puzzled V's over his pale eyes.

Lefty had not seen the approaching riders before. Two of them—and they were strangers to the Basin country.

The one on the rangy grulla was almost as

59

tall as he—a narrow-shouldered, wire-lean man with a mahogany-colored, expressionless face from which a cigaret burned seemingly unnoticed. Against his dark features his light gray eyes and even lighter brows made a startling contrast.

He was wearing a gunbelt, which was not unusual—but the butt of his weapon was on his off side as he rode up.

The man flanking him was a barrel-chested short man with a heavy, sleepy-eyed face, seemingly uninterested in anything save his own immediate concern.

'Howdy,' the narrow-shouldered stranger greeted him. His voice was soft; it was a feathery whisper, without volume. Lefty might have understood the reason for this had he been able to see through the dusty silk neckerchief hiding the man's throat; to see the deep-puckered old scar that time had drawn over a knife wound which had nearly severed his windpipe.

'Which way to Chuckline, fella?'

Lefty gestured to the southeast. He saw the man's gaze drop longingly to the coffee pot and he swallowed a narrowing suspicion and reacted with range hospitality. 'Light an' join us. The java's hot an' strong an' yore welcome to it.'

The lean man glanced at his companion and then nodded. 'Ran out of grub yesterday,' he said, as if apologizing. 'Be glad to join you.'

Bevans had come to his feet. He was standing by the fire, eyeing the two men. Now he turned to the pot, tossed the dregs from his cup and refilled it.

The narrow man slid a leg over his saddle as if he were tired; he let out a slow sigh as he slid down. Lefty, reassured, stepped back and turned to Bevans.

He didn't see the slug that killed him!

The narrow killer's Colt came out of holster in a smooth, silent motion—the half-ounce of lead slug smashed through the base of Lefty's neck and sent him sprawling across the fire.

Bevans, turning with cup in hand, stood rigid, shocked into nerveless inactivity by the suddenness of death. He saw the killer's Colt swing slowly toward him, his muscles cracked then as he dropped his cup and grabbed with fumbling, desperate haste for his gun.

The first bullet seemed to lift him back on his heels—the second jackknifed him into a limp, spasmodic huddle.

Through it all the barrel-chested man had sat saddle in sleepy-eyed disinterest.

The narrow man stepped to Lefty's side and rolled him out of the fire which had smothered under him. He looked down at the bodies, and his voice was callously casual. 'This one will do, Breel. Give me a hand with him!'

They picked out one of the two Hammer horses picketed beyond the wagon; they saddled and tied Lefty's limp body across it and sent the animal lunging away, spurred on by hammering shots at its heels. The bronc headed for Hammer, and it was where they wanted it to go.

They left Bevans where he had fallen. They mounted and rode through the canyon, and from the rock-strewn bench above Gaines Wobbly G spread they drew up and waited.

Below them, pushed up against the fringe of cottonwoods on the inward curve of the Salt, Canady's old shack lay in the morning sun. A thin plume of smoke rising from the chimney told them Ben was up.

They rode down toward the shack, and before they turned onto the hard-packed yard the door opened. Ben stood on the threshold, a rifle in his hands. He put it aside as they rode up, a welcoming grin on his swollen lips. He had discarded the bandages Doc Kedner had wound around his jaw, but one side of his face was still swollen, as though he had a bad toothache.

'Glad to see you, Cass—you, Breel,' he greeted them. 'Come in an' have breakfast.'

Cass, the dark-faced gunslinger, shook his head. 'No time. Need yore help. How many cows you got close by?'

Gaines frowned and scratched his beard stubble. ''Bout thirty head. Mebbe thirty-five. Down in the creek bottoms.'

'Any Bar L stuff?'

Gaines shrugged. 'Some of Mike's beef drift

up this way. Why?'

'We got a roundup on our hands,' Cass whispered. 'We're driving them through the canyon, onto the Strip.'

The burly rancher licked his split lips. 'Now? With two of Hammer's riders out there, stringin' wire—?'

'They're through stringin' wire,' Cass said thinly. 'They're dead!'

Gaines' eyes glittered. Then doubt blotted out the pleasure he had taken at this news. 'Hammer'll go on the prod when they find out,' he said slowly. 'They'll hit here first—'

Cass nodded. 'That's what we want, Ben. Hammer on the prod!'

Ben scowled. 'What am I supposed to do when they come? Buck Hammer alone?'

'Not alone. You won't even be here. Yore work's done—as of now.' Cass' eyes were lidded as he said this. Behind him Breel glanced away.

'Hammer'll come pilin' through the canyon after yore hide,' Cass continued—'an' the rest of the Dogbone ranchers. That's what we want. You'll be gone, but—'

'Mike an' the other fools will be home!' Ben finished. He laughed with pained, ugly pleasure at the prospect.

Cass swung his mount away. 'Let's get them cows moving!'

They did better than anticipated. They drove forty Wobbly G cows, four of Mike's Bar

63

L, and even two of Dutch Muehler's Rocking M beef onto the Strip, tearing down the wire Bevans and Lefty had erected as they moved onto Hammer range.

Cass watched them scatter and head for the nearest of the two springs, less than a mile away. There was enough representation there to fool Hammer; enough to lay the blame for the killing of Hammer men where Cass wanted it—on the Dogbone ranchers!

Later, from the top of Dogbone, hidden by jumbled rock and brush, Cass watched the shimmering reaches of the Strip with his field-glasses. Below him, in a small hollow, Breel and Gaines waited—the first with inbred patience, the second with a narrowing restlessness that sought outlet in periodic swigs from a fast-emptying whiskey bottle.

Finally Cass' long wait was ended. He saw a rider emerge out of the haze ... a lone man coming at a steady lope toward the dead camp of the morning.

He turned and signaled to the men below him, his face showing a brief smile that held the ruthlessness of a crouched cougar.

Miles North, coming in from the northeast, almost in a line with the path taken by Cass and Breel hours earlier, missed Lefty's cayuse on its way back to the spread.

He came down off the lower ridge facing Dogbone across the Strip. From the top of the ridge he had glimpsed Chuckline, far off in the distance—now, as he came down into the long narrow valley, Dogbone hid the town from sight.

On his left the black, desolate Diamonds sparkled in the sun. Flecked with quartzite, they reflected a thousand points of light . . .

He saw the cattle milling around the reservoir as he rode up, and his eyes narrowed, for he knew that not all of them could be Hammer beef. He had not yet completed the shift from the western reaches of Hammer of the promised thousand head he planned to graze on the Strip.

He let the black pick its own pace toward the water while he put his eyes to searching for the two men he had sent here. He saw no sign of them, but he could make out the wagon in the distance, and he thought, *It could be they're working in the canyon.*

But when he rode close enough to make out brands on the steers crowding the reservoir, he knew something had gone wrong. The Wobbly G stood out in careless branding on the flanks of most of them—among them he also made out O'Lean's Bar L iron. As he turned away, a Rocking M three year old moved out of the bunch into plain view and fell to grazing contentedly.

Anger settled in Miles like a driving weight. So the Dogbone ranchers had defied Hammer and followed Ben Gaines' lead? He forgot for the moment he had come out to make peace with them—he thought of Bevans and Lefty, and worry sharpened his anger.

He turned and set the black to a run, and came upon their camp almost before he noticed it.

He saw Bevans sprawled out by the blackened embers of a cold fire, a small huddle of clothes under the blazing sun. The coffee pot stood close at hand; beyond it a cup had spilled its contents into the thirsty ground.

Miles saw this, and then his glance ran swiftly to the rifle still propped against the wagon wheel, to the team grazing close to the ridge, to the lone Hammer bronc circling its picket line. That fact gave him momentary, short-lived relief—it was possible Lefty might have gotten away.

He searched the ground, noticing that two horsemen had come to the camp. Close to where they had stopped he bent to pick up three empty brass cartridges—his eyes made out one plain boot mark. It was the print of a man's right foot, and the heel marked showed the impression of a metal clip added to reduce wear on the outer side of the heel. Time and a sharp rock, perhaps had punched a small wedge in this clip—to an understanding eye it left an imprint as unique and definite as a label.

From the position of the empty shells, that heel mark defined the man who had used the gun which had killed Bevans. Miles locked that bitter information away in his mind and turned to the Hammer rider.

Flies rose and buzzed with disturbed annoyance as he bent over the man. The two bullet holes in his chest were plain. *Two*. The killer had fired three rounds. Had he missed with one? Or had Lefty taken the bullet and yet managed to get away?

Wariness rose in him—he stepped away from the body and walked to the wagon. It was Lefty's rifle, he saw. He didn't touch it. He glanced into the wagon and noticed that one spool of wire remained.

He stepped back and stood over Bevans and surveyed the ridge rising steep and brush-choked ahead. There was a drowsy stillness in the air that was at sharp variance with the violence that had struck here. The silence weighed on him.

He had come in peace to Dogbone—but he had come too late!

He had little doubt that it was Ben Gaines who had led the others in the attack on Hammer—yet even as he thought this, he had the uneasy feeling that it was too pat, too bold a raid—too unprovoked.

Little by little the pattern of the trouble prodding Hammer had been leading to this.

He bent and hoisted Bevans to his shoulder and walked with the body to the wagon. He placed the man down in the wagon bed, discarding the wire—he returned and covered

67

Bevans with a blanket.

The sun was hot in a brassy sky and the effort had brought sweat to Miles—there were dark half-moons under his arms.

There was nothing he could do for Bevans that couldn't wait; inside him was an urgency to see Ben Gaines, to see if the heel of his right boot had a metal clip with a small cut in it!

He drew his Winchester and laid it across his saddle as he kneed his black toward the canyon mouth. His eyes were narrowed and grim as he rode past the uprooted posts and the broken wire running in great tangles over the ground.

Plain in the gully were the hoof marks of cattle which had passed recently—heading for the Strip!

CHAPTER EIGHT

Miles came out to the rocky bench and looked down on the log and stone shack which had been Canady's spread and was now Ben Gaines' Wobbly G.

It was an unpretentious place, built solidly but plainly close to the north bank of the Salt. Canady and his wife had been people of limited ambition—a small garden, together with a few chickens, a half-dozen hogs and a few head of beef had supplied most of their needs.

Miles could see no change in the place since Gaines had taken over. If anything the place seemed to have gone to seed—it had an air of sullen resignation to the brutal beat of the sun. The corrals were empty.

The place seemed deserted. Miles studied the scene for a long moment, giving Ben a chance to make his appearance if he was at home. After what had happened this morning, he doubted this. Ben would not have remained here to face Hammer alone; he wondered if Gaines had holed up at Mike's place, with the others. They would be fools not to expect retaliation.

He rode down to the glaring, hard-packed yard, and as he approached he felt more sure than ever that Ben was gone. Yet the wariness persisted—there was something wrong about the whole thing which he could feel, yet not place. He wasn't satisfied with the apparent explanation of what had happened—

A big dog came out of the barn as Miles rode into the yard. He was a shaggy brindle with an old scar ploughed deep over his left eye. He watched Miles from close by with a narrowed, hostile stare.

Miles halted the black by the door. There were no windows facing him—only the blank, weathered panels.

The brindle came a few feet closer, and Miles' black turned to eye the animal with a wary regard.

Miles stepped out of saddle, sliding his rifle under his right arm. The brindle made a rush for him and he turned, swinging the muzzle around fast. The dog backed away, growling low in its shaggy throat.

Miles waited, his eyes moving over the area; he had the uneasy feeling he was being watched. The silence in the glaring yard had an unreal quality.

He called out roughly: 'Ben!'

No one answered. After a moment he flipped up the latch and shoved the door open. He stepped out of line, pressing himself against the building, not entering. It was an instinctive move; he was pretty sure no one was inside.

The brindle growled menacingly, but kept its distance.

Miles took a sharp breath and stepped into the house, moving quickly away from the open door.

There was no one in the big kitchen. Stale cooking smells seemed to permeate the walls—the rancid odor of bacon was most persistent.

A dirty dish with scraps of food and a cup lay on the homemade table. Flies buzzed around both. A coffee pot was on the stove—a greasy frying pan.

The first was not long dead—the coffee was still lukewarm.

But there was no one in the house.

Miles made sure of this by looking into the bedroom. Gaines, he noticed irrelevantly, was not a tidy man.

He came out, closing the door behind him. Mike's place was five miles down the Salt. His hand brushed down over his Colt; he hoped Ben Gaines was there.

It had come time to settle the question between them!

High up on Dogbone Ridge three men watched Miles ride out of Ben's yard and disappear among the cotton-woods.

Gaines fingered his carbine with sullen anger. 'Should have let me use this, Cass!' he muttered. 'You said Hammer would be headed this way. But Miles was alone.'

Cass Naylor's pale eyes were puzzled. 'The rest of them will be ridin',' he said. He could not understand why Miles had come alone, but it still didn't alter his plans.

'I could have gotten close enough to pick him off,' Gaines argued harshly. 'With Miles dead we'd have Hammer on the run. That's what the boss wants, ain't it? And with Red Shaner an' Sesta wearin' badges, we wouldn't have a thing to worry about—'

'Some day you'll strain yoreself, Ben,' Cass sneered, 'tryin' to do yore own thinkin'. How long do you think Shaner would keep that star if that happened? There's a better way to get Hammer, a way there'll be no kickback.'

Gaines snorted.

Cass' hand made a sweeping gesture in the direction Miles had taken. 'It's worked out the way we planned, Ben. Miles is Hammer, even if he is alone. He's got blood in his eye, an' he's headed for Mike's place. However it turns out down there, Hammer loses!'

He turned to the horses. 'Let's get back to yore place, Ben!'

*   *   *

They rode down the steep, narrow trail and hit the Salt where it fretted up close to the ridge and turned away, its sandy bed a glaring white in the sun.

Ten minutes later they rode up the low bank and came into the ranch yard, passing among the drooping cottonwoods and cutting around the barn.

The brindle came to meet them as they pulled up by the corral. He sat on his haunches as Ben dismounted. The blocky man had practically finished the bottle of whiskey and now the impact of the alcohol was affecting him, making his steps unsteady, his thinking blurred.

He almost stumbled over the dog; he bent and scratched the dusty ears. 'Don't like bein' left behind, eh?' he muttered. He pushed the sharp muzzle away with a playfully rough gesture and straightened, turning to eye the

72

two riders.

'Hey? Comin' in?'

Cass shook his head. 'We'll wait. Get yore things together.'

Gaines nodded. 'Glad to be leavin',' he mumbled. 'Good to get back with the boys—'

He walked unsteadily to the door. Something bothered him. He turned abruptly. 'What if—' His eyes snapped wide as Cass' right hand came up smoothly with a Colt filling it. Incomprehension flooded them—he was given no time for understanding.

Cass' Colt blasted sharply in the heat-filled stillness!

Breel sat lazily, a faint tightness around his heavy mouth. He had known it was coming; he had heard Brand give the order. Yet the utter callousness of it sent a faint distaste through him. He kept the look of distaste from his face.

Cass blew smoke from his muzzle, jacked two fresh cartridges into empty chambers.

His whisper was dry and false in the stillness. *'Vaya con Dios*, Ben!'

The brindle had jumped away at the shots. He faced the riders now, his growl menacing. Cass swung the Colt in his direction and the dog leaped sidewise and ran around the house, disappearing quickly.

Breel laughed sourly. 'Gun shy.'

Cass shrugged. 'We're through here. Let's head for town. The rest is up to our new sheriff—Red Shaner!'

CHAPTER NINE

The hot wind came through the willows overhanging the wet slick under the cutbank; it carried the quick sound of a woman's laughter. Miles reined in here and laid his glance on the house he could see through the willows, on a flat piece of ground away from the cut of the Salt.

Beyond the house, against a slope of brown earth, rows of stunted corn stood stark and bare, burning in the implacable sun—the stubby, burned rows seemed bitter testimony of Mike O'Lean's constant failure.

Mike's oldest girl was drawing water from the yard well. Miles could see her attention was drawn to the house as she worked the long pivot pole which raised the water bucket from the depths.

A yellow-wheeled surrey he recognized was drawn up in the yard, and Miles placed the voice now, wondering how long it had been since he had heard Cobina Kedner laugh like that.

He kneed his black into motion, through the path that wound through the fringe willows.

The O'Lean girl saw him ride out of the willows and head up the slight slope toward the ranch yard. She placed the bucket down and set the boards over the well top and faced him with a not unfriendly regard.

Cobina was on the shaded veranda, half hidden by untrimmed honeysuckle vines which swarmed over the support posts. Miles glimpsed the massive figure of Cathy O'Lean in the wicker rocker; he put his glance to a quick appraisal of the surroundings, but saw no sign of Mike or Ben Gaines.

There was a drowsy peace here, deepened by the murmur of bees around the honeysuckle; the fragrance was heavy in the hot still air.

He turned the black toward the house, and Cobina appeared at the head of the stairs.

Miles reined in and looked at her, seeing her tall, full-bodied figure in a new light that sent a little surge of wondering surprise through him.

Since his return to the Basin he had not really noticed her; now memories crowded in on him and he felt a stirring and a warmth, like a man who has come back from a long journey to the familiar peace of home. He felt this without being able to define it—then he was conscious that he was staring at her and that color had come up to enfold her welcoming smile.

He touched his hat then and said: 'Hello, Cobina.'

'Miles! It's nice to see you again,' she replied. Her voice was warm yet reserved. It was as though the long years they had known each other had been fenced off in some private preserve of her thoughts. 'I was just leaving. But if you're visiting, I'll stay a while longer.' She turned to Mrs. O'Lean. 'Perhaps we won't need to ask Dad to come out after all, Cathy.'

Miles remembered then why he had come here. He said: 'I'm not staying, Cobina. I came to see Mike.' His tone was short. He had not come to visit, and if Mike was about, with Ben Gaines, the meeting would not be pleasant.

His tone brought Cobina's eyes back to him in quick appraisal; her glance rested on the rifle he still carried across his saddle. He felt her sudden sharp concern and slid the rifle back into its scabbard and dismounted.

She stepped aside as he came up to the veranda, a tall, wide-shouldered man with hardness in the gray regard of his eyes, the tight clamp of his mouth. This was the change in Miles which Cobina saw, and she wondered again, with underlying pain, what it was that had changed the easygoing man she had known.

Miles swept his hat from his head and faced Cathy O'Lean. 'Is Mike at home?'

Cathy's high-colored, fleshy features wavered between uneasiness and deferential welcome. She said vaguely: 'Mike left this morning, Mr. North. I think he did say he was going to see Shorty—'

'Was Ben Gaines with him?'

76

She shook her head. 'No. Leastwise not when he left here.' She blinked up at Miles. 'Why? Is there something wrong?'

'I think there is, Mrs. O'Lean,' Miles nodded. 'But I would rather talk to your husband about it.'

Cathy O'Lean looked upset. She folded and unfolded her hands; her voice was querulous. 'I'm sure Mike will be back shortly. I do hope he is not with Ben Gaines. If there has been trouble—'

Cobina broke in quietly: 'Miles, why not wait for Mike?'

The boss of Hammer shrugged. He was thinking of Bevans in the wagon—the wire down in the canyon. Perhaps the thing had gone too far for talk now—it looked as though Mike O'Lean, and possibly the other Dogbone ranchers, had thrown in with Ben on this.

And the wry thought came to him now, as he considered this, that he had come back to Hammer determined to make it a big spread fast; blindly he had shut out everything which could not help him achieve this purpose. Now he was finding, instead, that Hammer was fighting for its life . . .

He felt Cobina at his side; it was a long time since he had been aware of a woman. And then he thought of Kate Barrow and knew he was being unfair to her.

Cobina said: 'You could help here, Miles.'

He turned to her. 'Help? How?'

77

'Tommy has a carbuncle on his neck,' she replied. 'It's ready for lancing.'

Miles frowned. 'That's your father's job, not mine. I'm not a doctor, remember?'

'I remember,' she said, 'although it is hard to believe. I remember when it was the only thing in your life, Miles—'

'A man changes,' he cut in brusquely. The old hurt was in him; his reaction was instinctive, an armor over the wound beneath.

She bit her lip. Her eyes were gray and serious as she looked at him. 'I'm sorry, Miles. I had no right to bring that up.' Her smile had its barrier of reserve; it had its own armor. 'I think I had better go after all. Dad will be needing me—'

'Where is Doctor Kedner?' Miles asked bluntly.

'In town,' she replied. 'I drove out to bring some cough medicine for one of the children. Dad had promised he'd drop by, but he's been busy with Baldy Simms—'

He nodded then, remembering. 'I heard about that,' he said. He turned to Mrs. O'Lean, filling her chair with a sort of helpless agitation. 'It's one of the things I want to see Mike about—'

The big woman came out of her chair, panting slightly with the exertion. She was a complacent person; she took things much more calmly than her husband. But trouble reached her now and upset her—

'Mike had nothing to do with that, Mr. North. I'm sure of it. He didn't even know about it until yesterday afternoon, when Joe Larsen rode over with the news about the sheriff and Baldy Simms.'

Miles smiled to reassure her. 'I don't think he did, either. But something else has happened since then—and I'd like to talk to Mike about it.' He made a slight gesture with his hand. 'I'm sorry I've upset you, Cathy. I think I can straighten things out with Mike. And while I'm waiting I'd like to take a look at Tommy.'

Mrs. O'Lean glanced at Cobina; she nodded. 'I'll fetch the boy,' she said hurriedly. 'He's probably hiding. I told him Doc Kedner would lance it when he came—'

Cobina paused on the steps. She watched Mike's wife disappear indoors. Her voice was worried. 'You think Mike is mixed up with the killing of the sheriff, Miles?'

He lifted his shoulders. 'I'm not sure. I only know that things have changed a lot since I came back. Hammer lived in peace in the Basin, Cobina. It's the biggest ranch here, but we always got along with our neighbors. But since my father left, there's been trouble. Most of it, it seemed, came from here—from the folks who used to be my father's friends. Now I don't know, Cobina.'

She nodded, sharing his problems, understanding a little about the trouble

Hammer had been having. She had heard people talk; she had listened to her father's comments. Doctor Kedner blamed much of it on Miles himself, on his chip-on-his-shoulder attitude since he had returned from Chicago. Cobina understood her father's attitude, too— he had been disappointed in Miles. The boy who had been his protégé, who had often followed him on his rounds, had come back a stranger.

She understood this and had not shared her father's disapproval; she knew that Miles had been having trouble with the Dogbone ranchers.

'Mike is hotheaded,' she said. 'But surely he'll listen to reason.' She made a worried gesture in the direction of the house. 'Cathy is frightened, Miles. There's been talk of range war—of killing—'

'It's already begun,' Miles muttered harshly. 'One of my men was killed this morning. The other is missing. That's why I came here, looking for Mike and Ben Gaines!'

She brought a hand up quickly to her mouth. 'No, Miles!'

'I had Jack Bevans and Lefty Conners building a wire fence across the entrance to the Strip,' he said. His tone was grim. 'This morning I rode over to tell them to take it down. I was going to make my peace with Mike, with the others here. I found Jack dead. He had been shot down, from close range, by someone who had given him little warning. Lefty was gone. Ben's cows, and Mike's, were on the Strip.'

His voice was bleak. 'What would you have thought, Cobina?'

She shook her head. 'Ben Gaines, yes.' Her voice was small. 'But Mike and Shorty and the others—I can't believe they would, Miles.'

'I've got to find out,' Miles said. 'I've got to know.'

He turned as Mrs. O'Lean came to the door. She was holding a wiry eight-year-old boy by the arm. He was hanging back, his eyes dark and apprehensive on Miles.

Hammer's boss smiled at him. He turned to Cobina. 'I'm going to need a nurse,' he suggested.

Cobina glanced at the big woman. 'I'm sure Cathy can—'

'Oh, good heavens, no!' Mike's wife exclaimed. 'I'm a baby when it comes to things like this. Mike ain't much better,' she added. 'Get's white all over even when he has to dig out a splinter.'

'We can't let Tommy down, can we?' Miles said to Cobina. He held out his hand to the boy. 'Stiff neck, eh? Makes you feel miserable? Can't get out and play like you want—'

Tommy hung back. 'It hurts,' he admitted. His eyes were shiny wet.

'Sure it hurts,' Miles said. For the moment he forgot he was the boss of Hammer, forgot

81

the worries that entailed. What he was about to do was nothing; it was a simple surgical operation that many families took care of themselves. Yet in this moment he felt strangely at peace with himself.

'I'm going to make it better, Tommy. It's going to hurt some in the beginning. I want you to know this. It'll hurt some. But a man has to learn to take some hurt when he has to—you understand that, don't you?'

The boy nodded and ran his tongue over his lips.

Miles grinned. He reached in his pocket and took out a clasp knife. He said: 'I'm going to give this to you, Tommy. You like it?'

Tommy nodded.

Miles turned to Cobina. 'I'll need some hot water and some clean cloth. And the oil lamp, please.'

While he waited he examined the ugly, white-tipped boil on the boy's neck. It was at the hairline, and he sympathized with the youngster, knowing how tender that entire area was, how even the touch of hair on that raised skin could be acutely painful.

'Do you have an apple in the house?' he asked the boy's mother.

She looked flustered. 'Some dried apples. Will they do?'

'One will be enough.'

She disappeared. Cobina came out to the veranda. The girl who had drawn the water

82

and two small children remained in the doorway, eyeing Tommy and Miles with button-bright interest.

Tommy's lips trembled.

Miles said confidently, 'It'll hurt for a few seconds, Tommy. Then it'll be all over. You'll be running around and playing before dark.'

He lighted the lamp and held the small blade of the knife to the flame. Tommy watched with fearful gaze. Cobina took hold of his other arm and smiled reassuringly.

Tommy's mother came out with a dried apple. She held it out to Miles and then fled back into the house.

Miles handed it to Tommy. 'Bite on it, son,' he said. 'Keep biting, even when it hurts. Remember, a man has to learn to take a little pain.'

Tommy put the apple in his mouth. Tears started down both cheeks; he blinked them back and bit into the apple.

Cobina said: 'It'll be over in a few minutes, Tommy—'

Miles cut across the white tip in a criss-cross pattern. Then he pressed his thumbs down on either side of the boil.

Tommy bit through the apple. He tried to squirm loose, but Cobina held him firmly. A muffled cry came through his lips.

Pus erupted from the crater. Miles wiped it away with wet cloth and pressed again until all the pus was gone. He wiped the neck clean.

Tommy was crying. Miles ran rough fingers through the boy's tow hair. 'It's all over, Tommy.' He wiped the blade and snapped it shut and held the knife out to the boy. 'It's yours.'

Tommy's fingers closed over it.

Mrs. O'Lean was in the doorway, looming over her other children as he turned. 'Put a potato poultice on it for a day or two,' he advised. 'Keep it clean. Might be helpful if you could snip his hair away from it, too.'

She nodded. 'I'll do that, Mr. North. I'm glad you came along. Tommy's been miserable with that boil—'

Her voice trailed away; she pushed her children aside and came out to the veranda. She was looking out over the yard, and her voice came quickly. 'It's Mike, Mr. North—'

Miles turned. The riders came around the corrals, moving up the slope of earth toward the house, riding past the dying corn. They came at a run and pulled up abruptly when they saw the big black by the veranda.

Mike O'Lean drew his carbine as Miles faced him. The sun bounced off the short, worn barrel, ricocheting soundlessly against the weathered building.

'What are you doing here, Miles?' His voice jarred against the stillness, thin and bitter with hate and surprise. 'What do you want here?'

CHAPTER TEN

Miles moved out to the head of the stairs. The dust stirred up by the riders was settling slowly, like a layer of ground fog.

His gaze sought Mike, leveled briefly on the rifle muzzling him. There was dust and sweat on the little man—and fear! He could feel it And that fear made Mike dangerous—it was like a hand on a hair trigger.

He saw that Shorty Baker and Dutch Muehler were with Mike. Not Ben Gaines. *Where was Ben?* The question asked itself, even as he saw the same naked surprise and fear on the faces of the other two.

'Where's Ben Gaines?' he asked.

Mike's hand jerked slightly. Miles saw the fear run like a live thing across the small man's thin face, saw the desperation in his eyes, and he lunged off the steps as Mike's rifle cracked sharply.

The bullet splintered the corner of the post near Miles' head and narrowly missed Mike's wife, standing before the door. Then Miles was down in the yard and Mike's next shot was wide, spoiled by the movement of his frightened, rearing horse.

Miles reached up and caught the rifle and twisted it out of Mike's hands. He brought the small man down with it, clawing at him as he

85

fell.

On the veranda Cathy O'Lean screamed . . .

Miles stepped away from Mike and whirled to face Shorty and Dutch. They had drawn their rifles, but they had little stomach for a fight. They looked down at the tall, grimfaced man standing over Mike and into the muzzle of the carbine Miles was holding. They dropped their rifles into the dust without being told.

'Looks like you knew why I came,' Miles said harshly. There was bleakness in his gaze, a sickening distaste. He had hoped the killing of Jack Bevans had not been of their doing—now he wasn't sure.

Mike came to his feet slowly. The fall had jarred some of the wind from him; the carbine in Miles' hand kept him from making any rash movement.

'I was never good with a gun,' he panted. 'Not like you, Miles. Not like the guns behind you. Maybe I should have listened to Ben more. Maybe we should have—'

'Maybe you should have kept on your side of Dogbone!' Miles snapped. 'All of you. Not gone starting something you couldn't finish!'

Mike drew a harsh breath 'We'll finish it, Miles! There's a new sheriff in Chuckline, not one bought by Hammer. You'll hang for this, Miles! So help me, I'll see you hang for killing Ben Gaines!'

Miles' eyes narrowed in surprise He looked from O'Lean to the two men still in saddle.

They were regarding him with the same scared attention Mike was giving him. They were afraid of him; they had been afraid of him even before Mike had tried to kill him.

'Mike!' he snapped, stepping up to the small man. 'What's happened to Ben Gaines?'

O'Lean brushed his lips with the back of his hand. 'He's dead!' His voice was a thin, intense whisper. 'You killed him, Miles! It wasn't enough that you warned us off the Strip. You had to fence us out. And then you came over and killed Ben—'

'I came over looking for Ben,' Miles admitted grimly. 'But I didn't find him. Hang it all, I don't care if you believe me or not,' he said, angered by the look in Mike's eyes. 'Just answer my questions! Where is Ben?'

Mike back away from the muzzle in Miles' hand. He licked his lips. 'Where you dropped him. In front of his door.'

'He's there now?'

'Yah!' It was Dutch who answered. His voice was scared. 'We yust left his place Ben was there—'

Miles cut in sharply: 'Mike, get into saddle! I want to see Ben. There's something I've got to find out. Something I want to show you—all of you!'

Mike balked. 'No! No you don't. You're not riding us out of here to kill us—'

'Don't be a fool!' Miles growled. 'If I wanted to kill you I would have done it when you took

87

a shot at me!'

Mike shook his head stubbornly 'I'm staying here.'

Miles' eyes were bleak. He held out the rifle to Mike, thrust it into his hands. Then he unbuckled his gunbelt, held it out to the small man.

'I came here looking for Ben and for you, Mike,' he said. His voice was rough. 'You want to know why? Because one of my riders, Jack Bevans, is dead. Because the wire he and Lefty were putting up across the canyon is down—and your cows and Ben's are on the Strip!'

'It's a lie!' Mike snarled 'You're trying to give yourself an out for killing Ben—'

'Ride with me, then!' Miles grated. 'See for yourself!'

'Yah!' Dutch broke in 'Why not, Mike? We go see—'

Miles thrust his gunbelt into Mike's hands. 'What have you got to lose?' he said angrily.

Mike licked his lips. 'All right,' he assented. 'We'll go see—'

*　　　*　　　*

Cobina and Cathy O'Lean stood together on the veranda and watched them wheel away. As she listened to the dying echoes of their passage Mrs. O'Lean said: 'I'm afraid . . . I'm afraid for Mike.

Cobina was scarcely listening. She, too, was

afraid—this violence was a new thing in the Basin.

'I'm afraid for Mike,' the older woman repeated dully. 'He's been dissatisfied here. I wish he wasn't like that. I'm not ambitious, like him. I've been happy with what we've got. I have my children, we have enough to eat. I've never envied Gail North—'

Cobina was staring toward the willows where Miles had ridden. She was thinking, prodded by Cathy's worried rambling, that this was what had changed Miles. He was no longer content with himself, with what he had, what he was doing. In a way he was like Mike O'Lean, growing bitter, growing hard.

Why? What had happened in Chicago to change him?

In a way she was like Cathy O'Lean, she thought—and she wondered if this was a virtue. She could have been content here in the Basin—content to be a doctor's wife, as Miles had wanted to be. And then, thinking this over, she knew it was more than that—she knew she would have been content to be with Miles whatever he wanted, as long as he was satisfied.

Mrs. O'Lean's voice held a thin edge of fear. 'I've never liked Ben Gaines He's stirred Mike against Hammer—he's made Mike dissatisfied. We always got along with the Norths before—'

Cobina turned to her. 'I think it will work out all right, Cathy. I don't think there'll be any

89

more trouble with Miles.'

Mrs. O'Lean shook her head. 'I'm not sure,' she said. Sweat was beaded on her fleshy, worried face. 'I'm not sure . . .'

*   *   *

The big brindle lay beside Gaines' body; he waited with the dumb patience of animals who have loved their masters and can't understand what has happened. He waited in the full heat of the day, a dusty scarred dog unmoved by the thirst growing in him. He lay with his head on his big forepaws, his tongue lolling, panting with the heat; a low, questioning whimper rumbled in his throat.

Ben Gaines had not been a kind man nor an easy master—he had lived a violent life and he had died the same way. But like many such men, he had a soft spot for dumb animals; he had treated the brindle as a companion and the dog had responded to him in kind.

The brindle heard riders approaching now and he came to his feet, his ears cocking menacingly, his eyes red and dangerous. But he began backing away, knowing instinctively that men on horseback could hurt him.

It had been a man on a horse who had put that scar over his left eye.

Mike and his companions drew rein several yards short of Ben's body. They watched Miles dismount and walk over to Ben. Mike's eyes

90

glittered with grim suspicion. He had Miles' gunbelt hanging from his saddle horn—he held his own rifle ready across his saddle.

'We didn't touch him,' he said. His voice bit harshly through the afternoon quiet. 'That's the way we found him.'

Miles hunkered down beside the body. Flies were gathered thickly around the blood drying on Ben's chest. The man's eyes were open to the glare of the sun—the odor of whiskey clung to him even in death.

Miles was thinking of the killer who had shot Bevans; he had to know if it was Ben. He lifted Ben's right foot, already stiffening, and let it drop.

Ben Gaines was not the man.

He stood silent, unmindful of the beat of the sun on his shoulders. He ignored the brindle's low, growled warning.

That's what they wanted, he thought bleakly. They wanted Hammer to come gunning for Ben and maybe for Mike—and something went wrong. So they killed Ben and left him here, after I had left—knowing that whoever found him would think I had killed Ben.

It was the only way this made sense. Could he convince Mike of this?

Mike's voice was thin in the heat. 'He didn't kill himself, Miles!'

Miles shrugged. He walked back to his horse and mounted and faced the Dogbone rancher.

91

'Neither did Jack Bevans,' he said.

'We can see Ben's body,' Mike rasped. His voice was stubborn; he had been friendly with Ben, more so than the two with him.

Miles swung the black around. 'I'll show you Jack's body,' he said grimly.

They followed him up to the rocky bench overlooking Ben's place, through the narrow canyon splitting Dogbone. They rode past the tangled wire, out onto the Strip . . .

Behind Miles, O'Lean suddenly reined in, his rifle glinting in the late sun. 'Hold it, Miles! Pull up!'

Miles held the black; he looked back at Mike, frowning. The small man waved his free hand. 'This what you brought us out here for? Into a trap?'

Miles turned. A half-dozen riders were visible now, converging toward them. They were close enough to be recognizable as Hammer punchers, led by Cud Walker.

Miles said: 'Wait, Mike! There's not going to be trouble. I promise you!'

The Dogbone ranchers held still as the Hammer men rode up. It was too late to make a break for it; they formed a tight, sullen group behind Miles.

Hammer's foreman drew up by Miles. He eyed the men behind his boss with distrust; his voice was sharp. 'We figgered you ran into trouble. Looks like we got here in time—'

Miles shook his head. 'I'm not in trouble,'

he said. Then, 'What brought you riding?'

Walker frowned. 'Lefty's cayuse showed up at the ranch, with Lefty's body tied in the saddle—'

Miles turned. 'Mike—you hear that?'

The small rancher nodded. Dutch said: 'Yah—we hear.' He shook his head in bewilderment.

Shorty Baker said: 'Who killed him, Miles? Who killed your riders—and Ben?'

Cud glanced from Miles to the Dogbone ranchers; his voice was sharp. 'What's happened, Miles? Who killed Ben Gaines?'

Miles explained what had happened, as he knew it. He ended coldly: 'I don't know who killed them, Cud. Not yet. But it wasn't Mike or Shorty or Dutch. It wasn't Hammer.'

Dutch spurred up to Miles. 'Killing! Yah—it was Ben who wanted trouble with Hammer, Miles. He kept all the time telling us Hammer didn't own the Strip—'

'Shut up!' Mike snarled. 'Don't go throwing the blame on Ben! We all wanted to believe that! And I still ain't sure Ben wasn't right. Hammer has all the available water in the Basin.' He eyed Miles and the Hammer riders angrily. 'I don't give a hoot if Hammer has a legal right to all this.' He waved his hand in a wide sweep. 'I'm not going to stand by and watch my stock die—'

'You won't have to,' Miles cut him off. 'Maybe we've all been a little hard-headed. It

93

worked out fine—for somebody. For the man who had Jack and Lefty killed—and Ben, maybe because he was through with Ben, or thought Ben might talk.'

O'Lean was a hard-headed man; Miles saw the angry doubt in the little man's face and he added harshly: 'Darn it, Mike, think! Someone killed Jack and Lefty, tore up the fence they had been putting up, and drove Ben's cows and a few Bar L steers onto the Strip. You can see for yourself—' He gestured toward the steers clustered around the reservoir. 'That's what they wanted. They wanted it so badly they tied Lefty to his cayuse and headed it for home. They could have left Conners lying here, with Bevans. But they were in a hurry. They wanted Hammer to think you and Ben were behind this—' His tone lifted bleakly. 'That's the way I judged it, Mike. So I went looking for Ben. He wasn't home. I thought he might be with you and headed for your place—'

'Who?' Mike's voice was a ragged, bewildered whisper. 'Who is it, Miles?'

'I don't know,' Miles answered. 'But I think this is only the beginning. It won't end here.'

'You're darned right it won't end here!' Cud said. 'Someone's gonna have to pay for Jack an' Lefty. We've been pushed around too long, Miles—it's time we hit back!'

Miles nodded. 'When we find out who to hit,' he agreed.

Mike turned and looked toward the rise of

94

Dogbone, blotting out the sun; he seemed to be seeking an answer in the lengthening shadows.

'Why, Miles? What are they after?'

'Hammer!' Miles' voice was bleak. 'It's Hammer they're after, Mike. They used Ben, and when they were through with him they killed him!'

Mike's conviction died hard. He said slowly: 'Ben was a friend of mine. I ain't sure—'

'He's dead,' Miles pointed out. 'I didn't kill him. Neither did I run your cows and Ben's through Dogbone.' He gestured again. 'Look at it my way. What would you have thought?'

'What you thought,' Mike admitted grudgingly.

Miles nodded. 'I made a mistake. I let Ben push me into taking a stand I didn't want to take. I was primed for trouble, but against the wrong people. Like you pointed out, my father always let you and Shorty and Dutch and Joe water your stock here during the dry spells. I'm not changing it.'

Mike stared at him. Dutch said: 'Yah—I never liked Ben's way—' He flushed at Mike's sneer.

Cud Walker said coldly: 'What are we going to do about Bevans? About the wire in the canyon?'

Miles edged the black around; he faced Dogbone, rising dark against the sky. 'We'll bury Jack and Lefty,' he said, 'and Ben Gaines!

And we'll put up the wire, the way it was before they killed Jack and Lefty—'

Cud frowned. Mike stiffened. 'You said we could use water—'

Miles was still staring toward Dogbone. His tone held a bleak conviction.

'So far I'm guessing. Carl Masters is killed. Baldy Simms was meant to be killed. The two men who have taken over in the sheriff's office worked for Wyeth Brand, a newcomer to the Basin, a man who showed up here shortly after my father disappeared, a man who supposedly runs a horse ranch in the Diamonds, but who spends most of his time in town.'

They listened. He went on, 'Canady dies, and another newcomer, Ben Gaines, buys the place from Canady's widow. Soon as he moves in he starts trouble—'

'Brand?' Mike's voice was thin. 'Why?'

Miles shook his head. 'I got a hunch it's tied up with my father—I got a feeling that when I find out why Brand's after Hammer I'll know what happened to Dad.'

Walker's jaw was grim. 'Give me the word, Miles, and I'll take ten men and wipe that horse spread out—'

Miles shook his head. 'I've got a better idea,' he said, 'one that will flush Brand out into the open.'

They sat saddle around him as he outlined what he wanted them to do—Hammer riders and Dogbone ranchers.

96

When he was through Mike said: 'We'll go along with you, Miles. I'll see Joe Larsen tonight. But—' He hesitated, smiling a little sheepishly. 'You'll be the one taking the long chance. If you're right; and Shaner is their man—'

'It's Hammer they want,' Miles reminded him. 'I'll take that chance.'

Walker's voice was harsh, underlining Miles' stand. 'I'll wait until tomorrow night, Miles. Then if you're not back—I'll come to town, with every Hammer man behind me!'

CHAPTER ELEVEN

Red Shaner stood in the law office doorway, a long, lanky hard-looking man frowning at the early morning traffic. He was an early riser. He had been born on a farm. Those early years had bred this habit in him, and later, as a cowhand, he had not found the early rising hard. It had not been this, or the long hours, which had dissatisfied him and turned him to a way of making a living which seldom required early rising.

Von Sesta was still in his bunk; his heavy breathing came through the closed door behind the cell block. Sesta was a night owl, at his best when the stars were out and the lamps were lighted. They made a pair, these two—

they had been together for a long time. They had been a pair when they had joined up with Wyeth Brand's outfit.

Shaner watched the swampers come out to the boardwalk and slosh dirty water from buckets into the street. A dog came out of an alley, sniffed at a porch support, used it—then trotted across the street and disappeared.

A few moments later the stage came around the corner; it rolled past the sheriff's office, heading out of town. The driver lifted an arm in greeting and dust settled slowly behind the churning wheels.

Shaner rolled himself a brown paper quirley. It was a new experience for him, standing here with a star on his vest. It was a lie and he knew it, and he wondered briefly how long the deception would last.

He was being paid by Brand, and a portion of that payment was in promises—promises of a bonus when Brand took over Hammer. All the men with Brand had come in on that promise—most of them, like Shaner, had their own private thoughts as to why the tall, predatory man wanted Hammer so badly.

'A thousand dollar bonus to each man,' Brand had said, 'the day I get Hammer.'

Shaner let his thoughts drift back to the day they had come to the Diamonds. They had taken over an old deserted shack in the foothills, built corrals, added a bunkhouse. They had built just enough to make it look to any casual visitor like what it was supposed to be. Brand had even registered a brand, the Flying B, at the county office.

They had been there less than a week when Brand and Von Sesta had ridden out together. They had been gone a day, and when they had returned Von Sesta had been sullen and Brand as touchy as a mean grizzly. Shaner had not been able to get much out of Sesta as to what had happened. Only the half-breed and Brand knew what had happened out there. But Shaner speculated shrewdly that it had had something to do with the disappearance of Farnum North, a man he knew only by name, and later learned had disappeared.

Now he stood in the early sun, retracing the events that had taken place since they had come to the Basin country—thinking of the moves Brand had made. Moves, it seemed, Brand had planned a long time ago.

Shaner had known Brand less than a year—most of Brand's men had not been with him long. But all of them knew Brand hated Farnum North—wanted Hammer. None of them knew why.

Shaner didn't dwell long on this line of speculation. He felt the heat of the sun against his lanky body and thought of the hot day ahead. After a while he flipped his butt into the street and went back inside the office. He stood in the middle of the sparsely furnished room, a tall, restless man, and the safe in the corner aroused his curiosity.

Masters had been without close kin, and his scant personal belongings were still in the two boxes piled in the corner. No one had called for them. No one had bothered to see what he had in that iron box.

Shaner squatted down in front of it. Instead of a dial lock it had an old padlock linked through an iron hasp. Shaner remembered seeing a key in the desk and went back to it. He found it in the upper right-hand drawer—a small brass key tagged with a little paper card marked SAFE attached to the key by a bit of red string.

Shaner walked back to the safe and opened it. The interior was bare except for a small cigar box holding sixty-five dollars in old currency. Shaner wasn't even tempted. Someone would eventually claim this for Masters, or whoever Masters had left behind. There was an envelope lying on the shelf beside the cigar box; a thick envelope with no name on it, no identification whatever. The sheriff reached inside for it and stood up, hefting it in the palm of his hand, wondering why Masters had kept this in his safe.

He walked back to the desk and sat down, settling his sinewy frame against the chair back. He could always say he had opened it by mistake, if questioned about it later.

One of the half-dozen enclosed sheets of paper was an old newspaper clipping.

He read it with casual interest, frowning quickly as his eye caught the names involved. He reread the clipping, whistling softly, then went on to the letter itself, penned in a straight up and down hand.

He read it with narrow-eyed interest, settling forward, hunched over the letter. When he got through he was sitting up, his green eyes glittering with strange lights.

For some moments he stood staring at the door, but his thoughts were moving fast, moving ahead to Saddle Pass and the Dune country; to where Brand and Von Sesta had gone that day, almost six months ago now. That was as much as he had been able to get out of Von Sesta, usually a confiding partner.

What he had just read cleared up a lot of things for him. He spread the last page of Farnum's letter out on the desk and examined the nicely detailed map drawn on it. He chuckled softly. A thousand-dollar bonus, Brand had said. Brand could keep his bonus.

If he worked it right, he could ride out of the Diamond country with a hundred times that amount . . .

He heard Sesta stir in the back room, and cupidity made him straighten hastily and slip the pages back into the envelope. He tucked it away inside his shirt, and as he stood up in that dingy law office the whole course of events had changed for him.

He could only conclude that this letter had

been left in the sheriff's care for Farnum North's son. The fact that it was still here meant Miles had as yet no knowledge of it. He had a sure hunch that Brand didn't know of its existence either. Other than Farnum (who he now knew to be dead), Masters might have known; perhaps Baldy. But Masters was dead—and Baldy was dying . . .

He remembered the role he was scheduled to play here, and it made him restless now where only a few minutes before he had almost welcomed the diversion. He would have to sit tight until his part of Brand's plan was taken care of; then he would slip away on some pretext, head for the Dune country and the money indicated in the map.

Von Sesta had awakened. The sheriff could hear him moving about in the back room. Shaner got up and reached for his hat and went out to breakfast to ruminate over the glowing prospects suddenly opened to him.

The day wore on; another cloudless, brutally hot day, rasping on tempers already frayed by weeks of drought. Friday. Farmers from the bottoms began arriving in town, some of them with small wagons of produce carefully nurtured and watered by failing wells. They would sell this on a high market, and later sit around and have a few drinks before going home.

In the late afternoon two men rode into Chuckline. They were comparative strangers, having been seen in town only once previously.

They rode past the sheriff's office. Von Sesta, his deputy's badge glinting brightly on his greasy vest, saw them ride by. He was standing in the doorway, picking his teeth with a broom straw. He made no gesture of recognition, although he knew the two men very well.

Cass Naylor laid his pale eyes on the deputy and slid his gaze away with the casual regard of a stranger. But his right hand dropped meaningly to his Colt butt, then up to thumb back his Stetson from his dust-powdered forehead.

It was a signal Sesta was expecting. He grinned widely as Cass and Breel rode on down the street, turning the corner for the agreed-upon meeting at Charlie's Bar. Then he closed the door behind him and went out looking for Shaner.

The next moves against Hammer would be up to the law—and the law, Von Sesta chuckled, was ready.

*   *   *

The shadows came away from the buildings and began stretching black patterns across Chuckline. The town was more crowded than it had been all week, but it was a sullen, temper-reined bustle that was like dry tinder waiting for the careless dropping of a match . . .

The bartender in Charlie's felt this as he lighted the overhead lamps—it made him nervous. He kept looking toward the back room where Charlie was; later on the big proprietor would be coming out to give him a hand.

There was a fairly steady turnover at the bar as men dropped in for a drink or two and drifted out. Several tables were occupied. At one of them Cass Naylor and Breel had settled and were engaged in a quiet poker game with a couple of townsmen. The stakes were light and the bottle on the table went down slowly. There was nothing in the pattern to indicate violence . . .

Von Sesta came in, shouldering the batwings, and stood for a moment just inside, his insolent gaze scanning the room. Then he drifted over to Naylor's table just as one of the townsmen cashed in and left. He settled into the vacated chair, shifting his gunbelt so that it remained easily accessible, a habit deeply ingrained in him.

Naylor nodded and introduced himself and his partner, and Sesta winked slyly behind his cards.

At the next table a party of dirt farmers were engaged in sullen drinking. Rough-handed, muscular men with red, creased necks, most of them from the bottoms—all of them found the long drought disastrous.

One of them, a young, straw-haired man

who only recently had married and staked out his quarter-section among them, was pretty drunk. He had had high hopes for his spread, and worked hard, and he was impatient and bitter with himself and the continuing bad luck he'd had He was an angry, quick-tempered man, and his voice was raised loudly above those of his companions.

'Let them fight it out!' he said harshly. 'Dogbone ranchers and Hammer! When it's over we little fellers here on the bottoms will get the water we need—'

'How, Lars?' the older man across the table from him asked bluntly. He was a deep-creased man with worried blue eyes. 'Does killing bring water?'

Lars laughed recklessly 'Maybe killing is what is needed to break Hammer,' he said. 'Maybe then we can get that combine Lawyer Atwell wants.' He pounded his fist on the table. 'That lawyer feller is for us little fellers. Greb. He talks good. A combine to bring water from the Cottonwood to the bottoms, for all the Basin to use—not just Hammer!'

'A dream,' Greb said, lowering his voice self-consciously. He was not drunk like Lars—he sensed the attention focused on them. 'For myself I think I shall go back to Nebraska—'

Sesta grinned. The Basin was rife with animosity against Hammer. There was little more regard for the Dogbone ranchers, mainly because they were underdogs—because, like

105

the bottoms farmers, they needed Hammer water to survive.

After supper Wyeth Brand dropped into Charlie's. He had a drink at the bar, had a few words with the harried bartender, and drifted over to the table where Sesta still sat and waited. The deputy finished his hand and rose, and Brand asked innocently: 'Room for another sucker?'

Naylor nodded casually, and Brand sat in Sesta's place and bought ten dollars worth of chips.

Cass dealt, his eyes meeting Brand's; he nodded slightly. Brand smiled. He ordered drinks all around and settled back to feign interest in the game. But his thoughts were on the long bitter waiting which was coming to an end.

Hammer was all but his. It should always have been his. It had been bought with his money, his and Big Al Moseby's. He had paid for it with twelve years of his life behind prison bars.

He thought of Al Moseby who should also be sharing Hammer with him. But Al was dead, with three posse bullets in his big frame. He thought of Al now, but it was not with regret; it was a fleeting remembrance only because Al had been with Brand and Farnum North in the deal, a long time ago.

Brand had had a lot of time to think in prison, and his thinking had settled and

106

warped itself into the groove of one objective, to get the man he believed had framed him; to make him suffer as he had suffered.

But Farnum had cheated him. Farnum had died a quick death under Sesta's guns—he had forced that killing to avoid the torture he knew was in store for him. And in dying he had laughed at Brand.

Brand's eyes glittered as he remembered. But he would have the last laugh, he thought grimly. He'd like to hear Farnum's laughter in hell when he took over Hammer—

There was a commotion at the next table where the bottoms farmers were grouped. Lars was arguing with the bartender who had come to their table. He wanted another bottle . . .

The bartender shook his head. 'No more credit, Charlie said.' He scurried away as Lars rose.

The older men beside Lars tried to hold him. 'We'll leave now,' Greb said. 'We have had enough—'

Lars shook himself free of them. He lurched to his feet and headed for the bar.

Von Sesta came back into the bar at that moment, with Shaner behind him. Shaner ignored the farmer and headed for Brand's table, but some devil inside Sesta held him by the doors, eyeing the drunken farmer.

Lars shoved his way to the bar and pounded on the counter. 'We spend all our money here, by Jakes!' he cried. 'I want one more bottle.

We will pay—'

Charlie came into the room, a big, quiet man. He wanted no trouble with the farmers; he had sympathy for them. 'Go home, Lars,' he said. 'I'll give you credit tomorrow. But tonight you've had enough.'

Lars put both horny palms on the wet counter. He was too drunk to heed Charlie's warning. 'Just one more bottle,' he said harshly.

Charlie shook his head and turned away.

The flat denial shook the man. He fumbled under his big overalls and brought out an old single-action Colt—a cumbersome weapon in an inexperienced hand.

'Charlie!' he yelled harshly. 'If my credit ain't good enough tonight, maybe this is, eh?'

Von Sesta pushed away from the wall. His dark face was alight with cruel anticipation. He had been idle too long; he was the kind of man who grew restless and needed this kind of outlet.

'Hey, Buster!' he called out softly. 'Drop that hogleg—'

Lars turned at the sound of this voice from behind him. He turned with his Colt leveled in his hand, and it was a mistake Sesta was anticipating. The men who knew Lars knew he had little intention of using the Colt, but the appearance was there, and it was enough for the grinning little deputy.

His Colt slammed heavily. The farmer

108

whirled around under the impact of the double slugs and fell across the brass rail; his Colt bounced out of his hand and skidded against a spittoon.

The small ringing sound it made lingered long in that stunned room—

Von Sesta walked up to the body, then turned to eye the white-faced men at Lars' table. 'He should not have tried to kill me,' he said. 'I am the law here. It is well for all of you to remember this, eh?'

It was Charlie who broke the silence. He came around the bar and stood over the body; then he looked toward the cowed farmers at the table.

His tone was kindly. 'I'm sorry about this, Greb.'

Greb stood up awkwardly. 'Lars meant no harm—' he began, then slumped at the look in Sesta's eyes. He whispered: 'We'll take him home. Is that permissible—?'

Shaner came to stand beside Sesta. 'It was a clean case of self-defense,' he said coldly. 'This jay was threatening Charlie. When my deputy called him he tried to kill him. Anyone here think differently?'

No one seemed to differ.

Sesta holstered his Colt and moved away, and Greb and his companions picked up Lars' body and left. Charlie went back to his room, a white-faced, shaken man, cursing himself for his cowardice, berating himself now for not having given Lars that last bottle. Better to have had him dead drunk than dead!

*   *   *

The night wore on. The killing of Lars emphatically pointed up the change which had come to the Basin, to Chuckline. There was law in town—gun law!

It was whispered that Carl Masters would have handled the drunken farmer without bloodshed; would have eased him and his companions out of the saloon without trouble. There was that difference between Masters and the new wearers of law badges in Chuckline.

There were some who argued that with the ugly trouble brewing in the Basin, a hard hand was needed. Von Sesta and Shaner seemed to supply that hardness.

But for the most part the killing of Lars shook Chuckline; it reached Mayor Gammison and brought uneasiness to him; it strengthened his earlier distrust of these two men. He decided he'd have to talk with Major Barrow—

Von Sesta waited with deadly unconcern as the night wore on. He and Sheriff Shaner were on the corner when the Dogbone ranchers came to town. They rode past without giving them a glance and headed for Charlie's.

Shaner flipped his cigaret into the street and caught Sesta's expectant grin. 'Let's go,' he said shortly. 'Here's our cue.'

They pushed through the batwings a few moments behind the Dogbone ranchers and drifted toward the rear of the room. Brand glanced at them and nodded and settled back in his chair. Naylor's grin was as cold as rim ice.

The Dogbone ranchers moved in a body to the bar; Charlie had come back out of his room to relieve his bartender. He faced them now, his broad face showing beads of sweat not all of which were caused by exertion.

He poured whiskey for them and watched their tense features. He sensed trouble brewing, and Charlie wanted no more of it.

Mike tossed down his drink and turned on his elbow, his bitter gaze sweeping the room. He seemed disappointed. He turned back to Charlie, his voice thin and impatient. 'Where's Ben? He said he'd meet us here.'

Charlie frowned. 'I haven't seen Ben since the night Miles and he had trouble—'

'I know,' Mike snapped. 'But I just left him. He said he'd be here—'

Brand heard Mike's loud voice; he glanced quickly at Cass, a sharp questioning in his eyes. Cass' face was cold, unbelieving. He was eyeing the men at the bar with cruel intensity.

Mike pushed his glass out for a refill. 'We'll wait,' he said. 'Ben will be coming in soon.'

Shaner caught Brand's glance and nodded. He drifted away from the back of the room toward the bar, a tall, sinewy, hard man with two guns thonged down on his hips. He said softly: 'Howdy. You boys having trouble with Hammer?'

Mike turned and looked him over, frowning a little. 'You the new sheriff?'

Shaner lifted his shoulders in a careless gesture. 'The badge says so,' he admitted coldly.

Mike's grin was crooked. 'Maybe you can help, then. Yeah, we've been having trouble.'

'Hammer?'

Mike nodded. 'They're putting up wire across Dogbone Gulch. Keeping us off the Strip—away from Strip water!'

Shaner's eyes narrowed. 'Heard you say you were looking for Ben Gaines. You been out to his place?'

Mike nodded. 'We left him about three hours ago. He said he'd meet us here—'

Involuntarily Shaner's glance went to Brand. He said thinly: 'You sure? You sure Ben Gaines was home—'

'Yah!' Dutch cut in. 'We see him. This afternoon. We ride through Dogbone Gulch to the Strip together—all of us. Then we see the wire. Ben wanted to tear it down, but Mike say no—he say we come see the new sheriff—'

Shaner licked his lips. He couldn't keep the sharp edge of confusion from his eyes; he had not expected this and it left him hanging.

'Reckon Hammer has a right to string wire

112

across the canyon,' he muttered. His voice lifted as he tried to retrieve the situation. 'Did any of Hammer's riders start trouble when they saw you?'

'No trouble,' Dutch said, shaking his head. 'They yust said, "Keep out!" We come to town to see you—'

Shaner shook his head. 'Don't see what I can do,' he muttered. 'Not unless they start trouble—' He started to move away.

Mike's angry voice stopped him. 'You mean we got no rights, Sheriff? You mean we can't get to that water on the Strip?'

Shaner turned, eyeing him with uneasy indecision. 'I'll have to check into it,' he said. 'I just got appointed sheriff. If you've got a right to Strip water, I'll back you, all the way!'

Mike's face darkened with pent-up anger. 'We'll wait for Ben!' he said harshly. 'He'll know what to do!'

Shaner headed for Brand's table. He caught Brand's slight head signal and turned away instead, heading for the door. After a few moments Brand rose, tossed his hand into the discards and followed.

The game broke up shortly afterward. Cass and Breel drifted over to the bar for a last drink. They glanced with hard-eyed curiosity at the clannish Dogbone ranchers. Then they, too, left.

Von Sesta, no longer grinning, was the last to go.

Mike curled over his drink, smiling coldly. His low voice reached only his companions.

'Miles guessed right so far . . .'

CHAPTER TWELVE

Brand waited in his hotel room. He stood by the window, a tall, stiff figure staring down into the black street. The sallow skin was pulled tight over a face marked by cold, barely suppressed rage.

They came in, Shaner and Sesta, Cass and Breel. They came into his room singly, casually, slipping upstairs unnoticed. They came in as puzzled men . . . They waited in that room, standing uneasily, eyeing that cold figure by the window.

Brand let them wait. When he turned, his eyes had a deadly glitter.

'What went wrong, Cass?'

The killer stood by the door; he spread his hands in a quick gesture. 'Ben's dead!' he whispered coldly. 'I killed him!'

'When?'

'About noon—mebbe a little later.'

'They saw Ben three hours ago, just before sundown.' Brand's voice was harsh. 'You slipped up, Cass.'

The narrow-shouldered killer stiffened. A quiet deadliness crept into his answer, a grim defiance. 'I said he was dead, Brand!'

Breel cut in, his voice urgent. 'Ben's dead. I'd swear to it!'

Brand's cruel gaze searched the two men, a puzzled light flickered in his eyes. He moved his shoulders. 'What about the rest of it?'

'Two Hammer men were stringin' wire across the canyon,' Cass said. 'We rode in on them, surprised them, killed them both. Tied one across his saddle an' headed it for home.' He took a slow breath, shook his head. 'That's the way you wanted it, Brand?'

The horse spread owner nodded.

''Bout noon we spotted a Hammer rider headin' for the ridge. Ben was with me an' Breel—we had tore down the wire an' run Ben's cows an' a few Bar L steers on the Strip. Rider turned out to be Hammer's boss, Miles. He saw what we wanted him to see, and he acted like we figgered. He headed through the canyon to Ben's place, an' he wasn't ridin' for fun. He didn't find Ben at home; he headed for Mike's place. We rode back to Ben's an' I killed him!'

Breel's heavy face held a frown. 'He was dead,' he repeated. 'We left him where he fell, in front of his door. Then we headed for town. That's the way you planned it—'

Brand snapped harshly: 'Not the way I planned it, Breel!' He walked away from the window to the small desk by the wall; he flipped open the lid of a cigar box. 'The way I

115

planned it Hammer would be riding roughshod over those Dogbone fools by now. And Shaner and Sesta would have a legal excuse to deputize a posse and smash back at Hammer. That's the way I planned it, Breel!'

The big-chested man said stiffly: 'We did what you told us to.'

Brand stuck a long thin cigar between his lips; his hand shook as he struck a match and lighted it.

'Something went wrong somewhere,' he muttered. 'Somewhere you and Cass slipped up—'

Naylor's voice interrupted; it was a chilled, deadly whisper of outraged pride. 'I said Ben was dead. Miles was on the warpath when we saw him. What went wrong happened after we did our job.' His lips curled. 'Someone lied in Charlie's tonight—'

Brand sensed the temper in the man and eased up. He knew Cass, and if Cass said he had killed Ben, then Ben was dead.

He threw up his hands. 'But why?' he asked. 'Why should those fools come to town with a story like that?'

Cass' lips pulled back against his teeth. 'I don't know. But I'm gonna find out. Breel an' me. We're goin' back to find out—'

Brand agreed. 'It doesn't make sense,' he growled. 'By all rights Miles and a dozen Hammer riders should be in town now, looking for the Dogbone ranchers. And Mike should have been here earlier, looking for the sheriff—'

Cass shrugged. 'We'll find out what went wrong,' he muttered.

He turned away and Breel, shrugging, followed; they went out silently. Brand chewed on his cigar. He eyed Shaner, slouched in a chair. Von Sesta prowled the room, his hand caressing his gun.

Shaner said idly: 'Miles might have caught on. He may have something up his sleeve, Brand.'

Brand paced the room; he turned and shook his head. 'Mistakes can happen,' he admitted coldly. He stood still, thinking, his eyes veiled by cigar smoke. 'If Miles bypassed Mike's and returned to Ben's place,' he muttered, 'he would have found Ben's body. He could have figured anything then.' Brand's scowl deepened.

'What I can't figure is what he's up to,' he added harshly. 'He could have gone back to Hammer to sit tight—'

'He saw Mike O'Lean,' Shaner cut in bluntly. 'He must have. Cass said he killed Ben—I believe him. That means Mike an' Dutch lied about seein' Ben. They lied because Miles told them to!'

Brand nodded. 'Makes sense.' A cruel grin twisted his lips around his cigar.

'It changes things,' he admitted slowly, 'but not too much. He can't prove who killed Ben.

117

And once we get rid of Miles, we have Hammer—'

Von Sesta whirled about; his dark face held a quick eagerness. 'Let me kill him, Brand! I'll make it look good—like that plough fella tonight. I'll kill him doin' my job—me, a deputy of the law!'

Brand shrugged. 'I figured on Cass doing the job.' His eyes narrowed. 'Shaner can hold things down in town. You follow those Dogbone ranchers home tonight. If they're up to something with Miles, you might find out something.'

Sesta nodded. 'I'll find out,' he muttered.

Brand was silent after Sesta had gone. Shaner got up. 'Reckon I should be gettin' back on the job.' He paused in the doorway, looked back.

'If Miles suspects who's been behind Ben, we'll have trouble,' he said. 'We'll have Hammer on our necks—'

Brand sneered. 'Let them come!'

*   *   *

The sudden soft snorting of a tired horse awakened Miles. He came up off his blanket with a gun in his right hand, his ear cocked for further sound.

A false dawn rimmed the eastern horizon, paling the stars. There was a chill in the air, an early morning chill that seemed to hug the ground like an unseen mist.

Miles crouched in the deep shadows under the cotton-woods behind Ben Gaines' house. He had been waiting for this sound, and his sleep had been tuned to it. Now he waited, a dim shadow under the trees, excitement driving the last vestiges of sleep from him.

He heard the clear ring of an iron shoe on a rock, then the soft snorting of a horse again. The sound carried clearly in the pre-dawn quiet.

Miles eased to the edge of the small grove. He had picketed his own cayuse far enough upstream to be out of the way. He had guessed they would be coming back here to check on Mike's story.

Ben Gaines, too, was out of the way. He was buried a half mile up-creek, in a shallow grave hidden by brush, out of sight of any rider making a casual search.

Crouched there in the darkness, Miles wondered briefly if Ben's big brindle still stood vigil by that unmarked grave. The animal had been skulking around as they had buried Ben.

A voice caught his attention, reaching across the stillness. 'Ben!'

There was no answer. After a short interval another voice, a thin, sibilant whispering voice, said: 'Dammit, Breel, Ben's dead! You and I know it. Mike was lyin', back there in Charlie's—'

A cold shiver slid down Miles' spine. They

had come back, the killers who had shot
Bevans and Lefty and killed their own man,
Ben Gaines.

The grayness of early morning pressed down
over the small ranch; it was more deceptive
than the night. Sounds carried clearly—the
creaking of saddle leather, the quiet jingle of
bit irons.

Ben's door creaked open. A few moments
later a faint glow flickered against the lone
window facing the cottonwoods . . . It moved
and seemed to disappear. Then a stronger light
flooded against the window, throwing its
barred pattern into the dust.

Miles paused.

A tall, thin figure came between the lamp
and the window; his shadow fell across the
pattern outside, then moved away. Miles made
his break then, heading in a crouching run for
the back of the sagging barn across the yard
from the main building.

He gained it without being noticed and
began edging along the side. His tall frame
merged into the shadow of the barn. He moved
slowly, silently, his Colt held down by his side.

The corner would place him at an angle with
the front door of the house—would bring him
into position to surprise the two men when
they came out.

He wanted these men alive. He had the
certain conviction that they could tell him why
Brand wanted Hammer—that they could help

clear up his father's strange disappearance.

He was almost at the corner of the barn. He could hear the tramp of feet as they moved about in Ben's shack. He could see the two horses bulking dark before the door, ground-reined and waiting patiently.

The stars were paling in the sky. At any moment daylight would push over the eastern rim of the world—the gray gloom would vanish. A cool breeze stirred against Miles' hard face.

Watching the front of the house, he didn't notice the roosting hen dug in at the corner of the barn. His foot came down on her tail feathers, and she woke with a loud, outraged squawk and went fluttering away, cackling indignantly at being disturbed.

Miles cursed silently and flattened against the side of the barn. The shadows were heavy here . . .

One of the horses, a rangy bay, turned to look in his direction; it nickered softly.

Miles felt the press of the rough boards against his back; he was surprised to hear his own harsh breathing.

There was a sudden silence within the house. The light went out in a quick puff. Miles strained his eyes to the door. After what seemed an interminable wait, a figure appeared in the opening, dark and shapeless. Starlight reflected coldly from the Colt in the man's hand.

The dark figure was silent, motionless, probing the gray gloom. After a while he turned and said to the man inside, 'Coyote, probably, Cass. Caught one of old Canady's chickens—'

He let the explanation fade into the quiet— he was not altogether convinced of it. The man who came up behind him obviously was not thinking that way, either. His low whisper didn't reach Miles, but it sent the broad bulk of his companion moving away toward the far corner of the house . . .

Miles came quickly away from the side of the barn. He had lost the advantage of surprise; if he let them disperse, he would be in a bad spot.

His voice lifted coldly. 'You looking for Ben Gaines?'

The killers whirled at the sound of his voice. Cass, nearer and partly facing in Miles' direction, brought his Colt up in a quick leveling motion and thumbed out two rapid shots before Miles' slug smashed into him, punching him back against the door framing!

The second of his two shots burned a gash in Miles' leg, three inches above his left knee. As he strode forward, the cut of the bullet made Miles stumble. He went down to one knee and leveled his Colt and caught Breel as the barrel-chested killer was cutting down on him.

Breel grunted under the impact of Miles' lead. He lurched away, dropping his Colt, and caught at the trailing reins of his frightened horse. The animal dragged him around as it backed away, pulling him out of the way of Miles' reaching gun.

In the foglike grayness Cass Naylor sagged against the rough framing, his eyes bulging with the effort of keeping his feet. He was fighting the terrible pain in his chest, fighting to pinpoint the blurred figure in the yard. His Colt seemed enormously heavy as he brought it up, thumbed out two wild shots . . .

Miles' return fire smashed into him, belt high. It forced a bubbly sigh out of Cass' clenched teeth. He bent over, suddenly very tired, and fell loosely . . .

Breel was fighting his pivoting horse. He had managed to get a fist wrapped around the saddle horn; with great effort he got his left toe in the stirrup. The bay was snorting, trying to shake him off so that it could run free. Breel's arm and shoulder muscles bunched in a terrible, concentrated effort; he pulled himself into saddle.

The move spent him. He fell forward on the bay's neck, instinctively entwining his fingers in the animal's thick mane. He was only half conscious as the bay, free of the drag of his weight, lunged away . . .

Miles was on his feet and moving toward them. He halted, let his Colt arm sag down to his side. His left leg felt weak under his weight; he could feel the warm blood run stickily down into his boot. He couldn't stop the man, and all at once he knew it didn't matter—he knew what he had to do.

He reloaded with strangely thick fingers which shook a little. He had never killed a man before.

Cass' animal had taken fright with Breel's cayuse, but it had calmed quickly as the shots faded. It had been trained to stand with trailing reins, and now it waited with dumb patience at the far end of the yard.

Miles walked to the body sprawled in front of the door. Cass was lying on his face, his boot heels up. The boss of Hammer crouched down and scraped a match on his thumbnail and examined the right heel.

The metal clip with the tiny groove caught and reflected the match glare . . . It seemed to reflect in Miles' gray eyes. The line of his jaw ran hard in the reddish light; he reached up to knuckle the wiry stubble on it.

'One of them paid,' he whispered bleakly. He was thinking of Jack Bevans and Lefty Conners—

Daylight cracked the eastern horizon as he straightened. He stepped over Cass' body and limped into the shack and found the lamp. He pumped water into a wood bucket and washed his wound. It was an ugly-looking cut, more painful than serious, the bullet had severed no main blood vessels, and the seepage was slow and already beginning to coagulate.

He made a flat wad of his clean handkerchief and bound it tightly over the cut with strips from one of Ben Gaines' old shirts.

The gray shadows in the yard faded; the yellowish dust took on a copper glow as the sun lifted over the low hills. Miles blew out the light and came to stand in the doorway. He debated briefly what to do with the body at his feet, then decided to let Cass stay where he was, as he had left Ben Gaines . . .

A half-hour later he was saddled and riding, a tall, grim man headed for town!

CHAPTER THIRTEEN

Red Shaner came out of the lunchroom and crossed the street, moving with an easy, loose-limbed stride. No one spoke to him, no one nodded a greeting. He smiled thinly, not caring a hoot about this. He knew the temper of this town was confused and afraid. But he and Von Sesta had been legally appointed to uphold the law, and the town was stuck with them.

He walked up the street, feeling the heat glare up from the powdered dust of the road . . . He walked past the barbershop and glanced in. Brand was in a chair, just having his face lathered . . . He met Shaner's eyes briefly, and there was a question in them.

That same question was in Shaner as he

kept on walking. Where were Cass and Breel—
and Von Sesta? It was way past noon and
Sesta, at least, should have been back earlier.

He stopped on the corner and leaned
against a post, his right hand lifting to the Bull
Durham sack in his shirt pocket. He wanted
Von Sesta back in town; with the half-breed
around he wouldn't be missed right away.

His green eyes lifted over the low roofs to
the far, hazy blue hills. The Dune country.
Impatience tugged at him. He clamped a tight
rein on himself; his hand was steady as he
poured tobacco onto flimsy paper, rolled it
with one deft twist of his fingers.

He saw Kate Barrow come out of the
millinery store and walk down the main street
and hesitated briefly before stairs leading up to
Lawyer Atwell's office . . . After a moment of
indecision she picked up her skirts and went
up.

Shaner brought a match to his cigaret. The
waiting was getting on his nerves. The play at
the Strip had misfired, at the moment Brand
was at loose ends, waiting for word from Cass.

He finished his cigaret where he was, a hard,
sorrel-mustached man making a harsh impact
on this quiet town. Families had been coming
to Chuckline all day in creaky wagons—men,
women and children. The men came for a
drink or two and to swap talk about the
drought, the women for the week's shopping,
the children for rock candy and cookies.

126

The regular Saturday night dance would be in the big barnlike structure behind the courthouse, but the merriment was subdued now. More disturbing than the drought was the pattern of violence that seemed to hang in the air.

Shaner flung his butt into the street and turned toward the office. He saw the rider now, a small figure on the trail and he came to a halt, waiting . . .

Miles North loomed up, big and solid against the brown stretch of country behind him. He came into Chuckline, holding the black to an easy gait, and the first man he saw was Shaner.

He felt the long regard of the man's narrowed gaze and he drew the black in toward the walk with sudden decision. Shaner straightened, his thumbs hooking in his cartridge belts.

Miles' gray glance measured the man, from scuffed, dusty boots to worn gray hat. He said dryly: 'New sheriff, I see.'

Shaner nodded. His glance held briefly on the ragged tear above Miles' knee and judged the brown stains on the pants leg correctly. Cass or Breel—or Sesta? He cursed silently, not knowing.

Miles' grin was edged. 'Tough job,' he said.

Shaner scowled. 'Meaning?'

'Last sheriff we had was shot,' Miles answered slowly. His eyes held an inscrutable blankness. He lifted his hand in a brief gesture. 'Wish you better luck, fella—'

Shaner's scowl was murderous as Miles pulled the black away from the walk. *How much does he know?* he thought grimly. How much is he guessing?

He watched Miles head up the street and pull up two blocks away before the stone-block bank. Some inkling of what Miles was up to came to him then. He cast a last glance toward the trail along which he had been expecting Von Sesta to come, then whirled on his heel and headed for the barbershop.

Brand was just getting out of the chair. The colored barber's helper was brushing his coat . . . Brand glanced up at Shaner strode in, caught the urgency in the sheriff's face, and pressed two bits into the Negro's hand.

Brand and Shaner went out together . . .

*   *   *

The gray stone blocks of the bank building still retained some of the early morning coolness. The green blinds were pulled down against the sun . . . There was an antiseptic cleanness that greeted Miles as he walked in.

There was a farmer at the teller's window; his wife and two children waited patiently in the small wagon outside. The teller pushed a few bills out to the man. His voice was kindly. 'Not much left in your account, Mr. Blake—'

Miles turned to the small gate leading to Major Barrow's private office. Miss Tinsey sat at a small desk, like a prim watchdog, guarding the way.

'Yes, Mr. North?' she said.

'I want to see John—Major Barrow.'

'He's out.' Her voice was stiff. 'He's gone to see Mayor Gammison, I believe.'

Miles hesitated. He could wait; he had to see Barrow. He noticed Miss Tinsey's disapproving stare and ran his palm across his beard stubble. He was suddenly conscious, too, that he had not eaten all day.

'I'll be back,' he said. 'Will you tell him to expect me when he comes back.'

The spinster sniffed. 'I'll tell him.'

The teller's voice came to him as he was turning away. 'Too bad about Lars, Mr. Blake—'

The farmer nodded. 'Lars didn't mean anybody harm.' His voice was tired. 'Me an' Maggie have decided to leave. I wanted to see Major Barrow about that—I wanted to tell him I wouldn't be paying on my loan. He can have my place—'

He turned away and saw Miles, and a look of fear swept across his weather-scoured features. His mouth clamped shut and he walked around the tall man and went out.

Miles turned to the teller. 'What's scaring him?'

Elmer Ross shrugged. 'Everything, I guess,'

129

he muttered. 'Especially what happened to Lars—'

'What happened to Lars?'

The teller told Miles. It was a second-hand story, as he told it—a story grown somewhat distorted with the telling. But the core of it remained true, and Miles saw now the pattern Brand had laid out.

'Von Sesta, eh?' he muttered. 'Shaner and Sesta. You say this Shaner had a letter of recommendation from the United States Marshal's office?'

'That's what I heard,' Ross admitted.

Miles' grin was cold. 'I'll be back,' he said softly, 'to see Major Barrow.'

Miles paused on the walk outside the bank. There was little doubt now in his mind that Shaner and Sesta were Brand's men, that they were part of the move Brand was making against Hammer.

But thinking this was one thing; proving it, another story. There was only one weak link in the pattern—Major Barrow. It was the banker who had practically forced these two gun-slingers into office.

Miles wanted to know why!

He mounted and rode down the street, and as he rode his glance lifted ahead of him to the far sweep of the Basin shimmering in sun. Dogbone ranchers and bottoms farmers—like Hammer they belonged here. They had existed side by side without trouble since Miles could recall.

Maybe his father's choice of a brand had been symbolic, Miles thought. Farnum had used Hammer to build in the Basin, not to smash.

He saw now that part of the trouble had been of his own doing. He had come back with a chip-on-the-shoulder attitude, and it had been easy for Ben Gaines to work on it. He had let an empty-headed girl shake him; let his bruised pride set up false values.

He had come back a sour, embittered man who had been aloof to old time friends—who had wanted to make of Hammer a power without regard for his neighbors.

And he had played into Brand's hands.

Brand was the owner of a horse ranch behind Hammer which no one had seen; a tall, predatory, quiet stranger to the Basin, who spent much of his time in town. The men he had with him were strangers, too—gunslingers. Men like the one lying dead at Ben's place—men like Shaner and Sesta.

It was more than Hammer that was at stake, Miles thought. With Shaner and Sesta wearing stars, and Hammer in his hands, Brand would control the Basin . . .

He was coming abreast of Attorney Atwell's office, and a sudden decision prompted him to turn to the walk. He tied the black to a support and climbed the stairs.

The rise of the building thrust its shadow

131

across him as he laid his hand on the knob and walked in.

*   *   *

Kate Barrow pulled out of Atwell's arms in quick embarrassment and turned to face the door. The color drained out of her face as she saw Miles standing in the doorway. She took a step toward him and halted; she felt a mounting terror and confusion in his grim silence.

She said: 'Miles...' and it was a sigh escaping her.

Faced with the inevitable, Ned Atwell found his courage. He and Miles were friends, they had spent pleasant evenings together. He had not set out to take Kate Barrow from him—the thing had happened despite himself. There had been meetings at church socials, at the weekly dances; occasional invitations to dinner at Major Barrow's house, sometimes in the line of business. He and Kate had discovered a lot in common, and the discovery had brought them close.

He stepped up to Kate's side now, his face tight, his lips bloodless. 'Miles, we should have told you weeks ago.'

'Told me what?' Miles' voice was even. He filled the doorway, dusty, unshaven, a bloody bandage showing through the tear above his knee. The big Colt on his thigh loomed

132

terrifyingly large to the girl.

'That I'm in love with Kate,' Ned said. 'That Kate loves me.' His voice was strained. 'I don't know how it happened, Miles,' he blurted. 'Believe me, neither of us wanted—'

'I didn't want to hurt you!' Kate said. She had never loved Miles; she knew this. And she knew, too, that she had wronged him: by being weak, by giving in to her father, by being frightened, later, of Miles . . .

Watching them, Miles felt a strange relief. It was an emotion he had not expected, yet he found himself without rancor.

I guess I didn't want to hurt you, either, he thought—*I think I knew all along we weren't in love, Kate.*

He shrugged. 'The real hurt would have come later, Kate,' he said slowly, 'if we both had gone along as we planned. I'm glad we found out now.'

Kate was close to tears; she had always feared the violence in this man. Now reaction brought a choking sensation, a relaxing of emotion, a thankfulness that was almost a prayer.

'I wouldn't have wanted it to happen to you, Miles,' Ned said huskily. 'I've felt like a heel for weeks—'

Miles' grin was crooked. He looked at Kate and his voice was light, chiding. 'This calls for congratulations, Kate—not tears. Ned—how about a drink? The three of us.'

Atwell nodded. 'I keep a bottle here— mostly for clients.' His explanation was sincere. Ned was an occasional drinker, and never drank to excess—he was not the type to drink alone.

He poured bourbon into three small glasses, and Miles, lifting his glass, murmured: 'To you both,' and drank his. Ned took a swallow, and Kate touched her lips to the whiskey and held back a grimace.

She quickly but her palm over her glass as Ned poured out refills. 'I never have anything stronger than sherry,' she explained.

Ned lifted his glass. 'To you, Miles—and to Hammer—'

'To all the Basin,' Miles amended. He looked Ned in the eye. 'That's why I came to see you, Ned. I wanted to tell you Hammer will back your combine—'

Surprise laid its imprint on Ned's handsome face.

Miles lifted his glass. 'To the future of the Basin, Ned.' He drank his shot and put down the glass and turned to Kate. He put his big hands on her arms and drew her to him; his voice was gentle. 'Congratulations to you both,' he said and kissed her.

There was no stiffening, no withdrawal in her—her lips were soft and grateful and her eyes were misty. He turned and walked out, closing the door behind him.

CHAPTER FOURTEEN

Von Sesta heard a low growling as he swung his cayuse away from the dry cut of the Salt. He reined in sharply and his right hand came up swiftly with a Colt filling it. He faced the sound, peering through the screening brush with alert intentness.

He heard the low rumble again, a warning vibration that brought a sudden narrowing of his beady eyes. He kneed his nervous mount into the brush, forcing a passage through it, and a moment later he broke into a small clearing.

Ben's brindle dog backed away from the rider. He had been crouched by a small mound of freshly spaded earth, piled high with rocks. The fur on the back of his neck ruffled ominously as he eyed the deputy.

Von Sesta's eyes glittered; his Colt came up fast and bucked in his palm. The dog had moved with the motion, but the slug caught him in midair; the impact sent him somersaulting. A second shot stilled his quivering body.

Von Sesta dismounted. He walked to the unmarked grave and toed one of the stones, but he didn't disturb it. He knew what had happened to Ben Gaines now . . .

After a speculative moment he went back to

his cayuse, mounted, and rode to Ben's spread.

He came to the Wobbly G less than fifteen minutes after Miles' departure. He rode warily his gaze picking up the crumpled figure in front of the door long before he showed himself. Convinced after a careful survey of the premises that no one else was present, he rode on into the yard.

A rooster strutted out of the sagging barn, balanced himself on one foot and watched the rider with an unconcerned stare. After a moment he flapped his wings and crowed—but he was an hour late to greet the dawn.

The deputy dismounted, bent over Cass Naylor, turned the gunman over on his back. He hunkered down by the body and studied it, picking at his teeth with the small blade of his knife.

He had always been convinced that this narrow-shouldered killer had been overrated by Brand. Now he was sure of it.

Finally he came to his feet and put the knife away. A nocturnal man, he had spent the night following the Dogbone ranchers home, and he had learned nothing from their actions. His patience failing, he had turned to make a swing this way before heading back to town.

He thought of Brand's elaborate planning. To him it was a waste of time. Brand wanted Hammer, and Miles North was Hammer. And to Von Sesta's way of thinking, the quickest way to get what one wanted was to kill for it.

Brand had wanted public opinion with him when he smashed Hammer. Von Sesta didn't give a hang about public opinion. The only thing he respected was a faster gun—and he had not yet looked into the muzzle of one faster than his own.

Cass and Breel had obeyed Brand's orders, and look what had happened! The small deputy grinned sourly. They had walked into a trap—a trap baited by a lie. Cass was dead. And Sesta had a grim hunch Breel had not escaped with a whole skin.

He studied the hard-packed earth for a few moments, judging the possible angle of fire which had dropped Cass. He could pick out no plain markings in this hard ground, but he walked toward the barn, where the earth was softer, and smiled thinly as he saw what he was after. From here he followed Miles' trail to the cottonwoods, and the rest was easy. When he came back and swung up into saddle he had learned that only one man had waited here for Cass and Breel.

He was pretty certain that man had been Miles North.

The deputy's eyes had a calculating glitter Miles seemed headed for town. Possibly the boss of Hammer had learned something here—either from Cass, before the man died, or from the missing Breel, to send him after Brand. At any rate, he had to get back to warn Brand what had happened.

He caught Cass' grazing horse and brought it back by the body. It took only a few minutes to get Naylor across his saddle and lashed down.

An idea was growing in his head as he headed away from Ben's spread, leading the burdened horse; an idea that brought a grim chuckle to his lips.

He would prove to Brand that the gun was the quickest way to Hammer. And the body riding behind him would be his excuse!

*   *   *

He made no effort to overtake Miles. He swung wide of the wagon road and kept to the coulees and the low hills... He had his reasons. He wanted to be sure Miles did not see him.

And because of this he ran into Breel.

He saw the burdened horse grazing along the banks of the arroyo shortly after he dipped into it. He slid his rifle out in a quick, easy motion and laid it across his mount's neck; then, as he moved closer, he recognized the heavy-shouldered figure slumped forward in the saddle.

He slid the rifle back and spurred his horse alongside.

Breel was barely conscious. He had lost a lot of blood and was clinging weakly to his saddle horn. One hand was still entwined in the bay's

138

mane.

Sesta leaned out and put a hand on Breel's shoulder. The gunslinger roused at the touch; he lifted his heavy frame erect and unreasoningly clawed at his empty holster.

'Easy,' Sesta growled. 'It's me—Sesta!'

Breel tried to focus his pained gaze. His whole body seemed on fire. His lips were cracked. He tried to speak, but his mouth was dry as tinder. Finally he croaked: 'Water—'

Sesta held his canteen to Breel's lips, supporting him with his right arm about his shoulders. The man swayed. He pulled his mouth away, and water made little runnels through the dust caking his face.

He said: 'Ran into ambush—Ben's place. Cass dead—'

Sesta nodded. 'Cass was a fool,' he said unsympathetically. 'He should have killed Miles when he had the chance.'

Breel nodded weakly. 'Way I felt. Didn't like—what we did—to Ben. But Cass—Brand's orders—'

Sesta shrugged. He knew it had been Brand's orders; he knew, too, he would not make Cass' mistake.

'You hang on,' he growled. 'I'll get you to a doctor in town.'

Breel sagged. 'Never should have gone back,' he muttered. His mind was still grooved in the happenings of the morning. 'Cass wanted to prove—'

He ran out of breath, out of apologies. He closed his eyes and hung on. He felt the jolting as the animal under him broke into a trot, and he put his ebbing will to one thing; to hold on until he reached town.

They came into town a full hour behind Miles. Von Sesta rode down the street, a sneer pulling hard at his lips at the commotion his appearance caused.

He took the corner to Doc Kedner's office and a small crowd followed him as he tied up at the hitchrack next to the flight of stairs. Dismounting, he drew his Colt and requisitioned a couple of gaping-mouth onlookers to carry Breel upstairs.

He went up ahead of them, kicked the office door open, and stepped inside, his Colt in his hand, and grinned at the doctor's startled regard. Doctor Kedner was kneeling by a boy in a chair, bandaging a bare foot. A wash basin tinged with blood was at his side.

'Got a customer, Doc!' Sesta sneered. 'He's got a hole in him, too.'

Harry Kedner straightened. He stared silently as the two men came in with Breel groaning between them. He made a quick motion to the leather-covered table by the window. 'Over there,' he said tonelessly.

They carried Breel to the table, laid him down and stood staring at their blood-stained hands.

Sesta made a directional motion with his

Colt. 'What are you jaspers waiting for—a tip?'

They scuttled out. Sesta kicked the door shut behind them and turned back to the doctor. Then his glance lifted to the girl coming into the office from a back room.

'Glad you're here, Sis,' he welcomed her insolently. 'Breel's gonna need a nurse.'

Cobina ignored him. She came to her father's side, and Kedner snapped: 'Put that gun away, Deputy. I'm a doctor. I'll take care of your friend. But I don't need to be threatened—'

'You'll take care of him all right!' Sesta butted in. 'Awful good care of him, Doc. If you pull him through I'll see you get a bonus. If you let him die—'

Kedner stiffened. 'If he dies?'

'I'll see his soul has company in hell!' Sesta's tone was brutally frank.

Kedner's temper kindled. He had never been a tactful man. 'You fool! Who do you think you are, threatening—?'

'Me?' Sesta interrupted insolently. 'I'm the law, Doc, duly appointed and sworn in.' He came up to the angry doctor and prodded him in the chest with the muzzle of his Colt. 'Get that, Doc! I'm the law—'

Cobina pulled at her father's arm. 'Dad—don't antagonize him.'

Sesta leered at her. 'You got sense, *chiquita*.' He nodded to Breel. The wounded man's breathing was harsh in the momentary quiet.

'Better take a look at him, Doc.'

Harry Kedner turned to the wide-eyed boy pressed back in the chair. 'Come back tomorrow, Pete,' he said gruffly. 'I'll take another look at it. And stay away from rusty nails—'

He waited until the boy had limped out; then he walked over to the table. He motioned to his daughter. Together they stripped the clothes away from Breel's chest.

Miles' bullet had smashed into the big man's shoulders, just under the collar bone. It was still in the man.

Kedner made a quick examination. 'I'll have to probe for it,' he muttered. He turned to Sesta. 'How did it happen?'

'In the line of duty,' Sesta said, grinning widely. 'Just an innocent citizen, ridin' to visit his friend—'

Harry's skeptical tone was impatient. 'Who shot him?'

'Miles North!' Sesta sneered at the look on Harry's face. 'The big bad boss of Hammer, Doc! The gent who's responsible for all the trouble in the Basin!'

He spun the cylinder of his Colt, conscious of the effect it had on the man and the girl; his grin was wide on his oily face as he sleeve-rubbed his badge.

Cobina watched him from across the table; her face white as a sheet. She watched the little catfooted killer swagger to the door, turn,

142

wave.

'I'll be back, Doc. Remember what I said— about him.' He gestured to Breel.

They watched him saunter out—a little brown-faced man made big by the gun on his hip.

Doctor Kedner's shoulders sagged. 'Miles!' he said wearily. 'So it's come to this—'

Cobina dropped Breel's bloodstained clothes; she cut around the table and ran for the back room.

Her father's tone was demanding: 'Where are you going?'

'To warn Miles!' she flung back. 'I know he's in town—I saw him ride by while I was at Garvey's!'

Kedner lifted an arm. 'I need you here. This man—' But she was gone. He stood in the office, alone now, with Breel's rasping breathing in his ears. It sounded like Baldy's breathing, just before the deputy had died . . .

The crowd was thick around Cass' body as Sesta came down the stairs. He saw Red Shaner and Wyeth Brand round the corner and come toward him, followed by several hesitant women. He waited until they were at the edge of the group before stepping off the last step and pushing toward them.

'Breel's upstairs with a bullet in him,' Sesta said. 'I found him an' Cass. Cass is dead.'

Shaner shoved his way through the group to the dead man. He turned then, his tone loud.

'One of Ben Gaines' friends. I met him last night—he was looking for Ben.' He frowned. 'Where did you find him, Von?'

Sesta grinned. 'Up at Ben's place—'

Brand pushed his way forward. 'What happened, Deputy?' His tone was significantly sharp, and Sesta took the cue.

'Looks like Hammer's out for trouble, Mr. Brand. These two friends of Ben's were in Charlie's Bar last night. I think you remember them.' He kept his face straight as Brand nodded soberly. 'They ran into an ambush. The fella upstairs said it was Miles North an' a couple of Hammer riders—'

'North!' Brand made a quick gesture. 'You sure, Deputy? He rode into town a while back—alone.'

'That's what the gent upstairs says,' Sesta repeated.

Walter Ferance, a tall, gaunt-bodied man who owned the mercantile store just across the street, had come to stand beside Brand. He was one of the county commissioners who had assented to Shaner's and Sesta's appointments.

He put in a weak protest. 'Doesn't seem like Miles,' he said. 'I can't believe he'd go that far—'

'You never can tell how far a man will go when he's prodded enough,' Shaner cut in thinly. He put his hands on his guns, his eyes glinting dangerously. 'This Miles hombre has been gettin' too big for his saddle. I heard his

144

pop was a right peaceable man—but his son seems to be tryin' to throw a long shadow, gents. He's started by tryin' to run the Dogbone ranchers off the Salt—he'll want the whole Basin next. Masters tried to stop him, I hear—and you all know what happened to him!'

There was a low, confused mumble from the crowd. Someone said: 'Killing never settles anything—'

'There won't be any more killing!' Shaner rapped out. 'Not by Hammer. Not as long as I'm wearin' this star.'

He turned to Sesta. 'Last time I saw Miles he was headed for the bank—'

The deputy grinned.

The crowd parted as the pair moved away. There was a deep, uneasy silence.

Walter Ferance licked his lips. 'I don't like it,' he said. 'I don't understand Miles ambushin' these men. We never had that kind of trouble before—'

He turned and walked away, urgency lengthening his stride.

Behind him Brand reached in his pocket for a thin cigar. He had given Sesta and Shaner a cue, and they had taken it from there.

Maybe Miles North had outsmarted himself, after all . . .

CHAPTER FIFTEEN

The late afternoon sun slanted through the cretonned west windows in Mayor Gammison's parlor and laid a pattern across Major Barrow's tailored legs. He was standing by the round mahogany table holding an oval-shaped tintype of the mayor and his wife in an ornate gilt frame. The heavy double doors leading to the hall were closed; he and Calvin Gammison were alone in the quiet, brocaded room.

The mayor shook his head. He was a short, round-bodied man in his late fifties, almost entirely bald, with only a fringe of white hair over his small pink ears. The news of Lars' death still weighed heavily on him.

'I know we needed someone to take over in Masters' place,' he repeated. 'But these men—these killers!' He shook his head again. 'We need order, John. I agree we need a firm hand to uphold the law. But what happened last night—'

Major Barrow interrupted stiffly! 'What happened last night was done in self-defense, Cal. A dozen witnesses will swear to it.'

'Did you see it?' The mayor's tone was sharp.

'No. But I heard it from the sheriff. From Wyeth Brand—'

Gammison sighed. 'Shaner and this itchy-fingered deputy—they worked for Brand, didn't they? Doesn't it strike you that he would very probably back them up?' He stood up now and faced Barrow across the heavy table. 'Who are they, anyway? Who is this Wyeth Brand? Is he a friend of yours, John?'

Major Barrow hesitated. 'I met him—before I came here. Shaner, too.' His explanation was forced.

Gammison frowned. 'I don't like it, John. I'm sorry now I agreed to their appointment. If you hadn't—'

'Carl Masters was dead!' Barrow reminded him grimly. Faint beads of sweat glistened on his forehead. 'Baldy was dying. We had a range war brewing on our hands. Creeping Jehoshophat, Cal—was there anyone else willing to take over in Masters' place?'

The mayor shook his head. 'I don't know. We didn't take time to find out. It seemed a good idea at the time. But it was on your say-so, John. You told us you knew these men—you said this Shaner fellow had worked as a United States Marshal—'

'You saw his letter,' Barrow snapped.

'I saw it,' Gammison admitted coldly. 'But I'm not convinced now, not after last night. I sent a wire to the United States Marshal's office asking about Shaner—'

Barrow stiffened, shock graying his face. *You what?'*

'I mentioned you in it,' Gammison

147

continued sharply. 'I asked for verification. I described Shaner—'

Barrow stepped to the table, leaned his weight on his hands. 'You had no call to do that!' he snarled. 'You had my word!'

Gammison stepped away from the man, frowning. He had always known the Major to be a quiet, dignified man, seldom shaken, never loud. Now he saw anger and desperation in the man's eyes, and a flash of understanding made him frown.

'Good Lord, man!' he exclaimed. 'What are you afraid of, John? What have you gotten yourself into?'

Major Barrow pulled himself together with an effort. 'It's not fear,' he said harshly. 'It's you. It's this checking up without my knowledge. It's your lack of faith in me, Cal. I looked on you as my friend.'

Gammison said kindly: 'We are still friends. But maybe you were wrong about Shaner. Maybe we've taken a tiger into the house, to catch a mouse—'

'Save the high-blown oratory for your campaigns, Mayor!' Barrow sneered.

Anger darkened Gammison's round face. 'All right, John. I'll put it in plain words. I don't like Shaner and Sesta. I think we made a bad mistake. They're gunmen. Worse—they're killers! I've had time to think—time to do a lot of worrying. But mostly time to think. And I've found that the trouble started soon after

148

Farnum North disappeared. It started along about the time this Wyeth Brand showed up in town—a stranger who says he's started a horse spread in the Diamonds. He spends most of his time in town, however. He's quiet and gives no trouble—but he's hardly sociable. And the men he says are his riders are men like Sesta—gunmen!'

Barrow snorted. 'Hammer riders pack guns, too—'

'I know those riders,' Gammison said, flushing. 'They're not strangers.' He lifted his hand as Barrow started to speak. 'Hear me out, John. The trouble between the Dogbone ranchers and Hammer started after Brand came to the Basin; after another newcomer, Ben Gaines, took over Canady's place. It broke loose the night Miles came to town looking for Ben.' He rubbed a hand thoughtfully across his jaw. 'Funny, isn't it, John, that Masters and Baldy were shot that same night—right after Carl had warned both outfits—'

'Maybe it isn't so funny!' Barrow interrupted harshly. 'Maybe Miles thought it was time to get Masters out of his way—'

Gammison stared. There was shock in his eyes. 'John! You don't mean that! Why, man—Miles will soon be your son-in-law! You can't believe that!'

Barrow straightened. He felt trapped; he felt sick. He had nothing against Miles, but he was a man at bay—he knew what Brand could do to him. And he knew he couldn't face the town, or his daughter, when that happened— he couldn't start over again.

'I don't know, Cal,' he mumbled. He turned to the window and mopped his forehead. 'I don't know what to think.'

'Miles didn't kill Masters,' Gammison said. 'Neither did his foreman, Walker. They left town right after Masters talked to them in the Green Front.' His tone hardened. 'Neither did the Dogbone ranchers have anything to do with it. Ben was in no shape for anything that night—the others took him home. No, John— someone else shot Baldy and Carl. I think you know who did. I think you know why.'

Barrow whirled. 'That's an outrageous accusation. Cal! I didn't even know there had been a shooting—'

The knock on the door interrupted them. Barrow choked back his words, turning. Gammison said sharply: 'Yes, come in.'

The doors parted. Mrs. Gammison, a frail, white-haired woman, said apologetically: 'Calvin, Mr. Ferance is here—'

Walter Ferance bustled past her, too upset to be aware of his rudeness. Gammison said: 'Thank you, Mary. You can leave us alone now.'

The storekeeper waited until the doors closed; he glanced from Barrow to the frowning mayor. His voice shook. 'We're in for it, Cal. More trouble. Terrible trouble.' He mopped his face with a blue polka-dot
150

handkerchief.

'What's happened now?' Gammison's voice was quick.

'Shaner and Sesta. They're looking for Miles North! They're going to kill him!' He took a long breath. 'Sesta rode into town with two men—one dead, the other with a bullet in him. He says they were Ben Gaines' friends—that they were ambushed by Miles and some of his riders when they went to visit Ben—'

Gammison sank back in his chair. He looked at Barrow, his eyes accusing. 'A tiger in town—' he said dully. 'That's what we've done, John.'

Ferance licked his lips. 'If they kill Miles, Hammer will tear this town apart, Cal—'

Barrow whirled on them. 'Don't try to lay it all on me!' he snarled. 'You appointed them, remember? If Brand takes over this town—' He caught himself on the verge of saying too much.

'I'll be at the bank!' he flung back over his shoulder. 'No telling what will happen now!'

He pulled the doors open, strode down the hall, plucked his hat from the hall tree. The door slammed softly behind him. In the quiet that came in its wake Mary Gammison's high-button shoes made a soft scuffing as she came into the parlor. There was bewilderment on her thin face.

'Calvin—is something wrong?'

Gammison didn't answer her. He sat

151

slumped in his chair, staring at Ferance, but he didn't really see the gaunt, worried storekeeper. He was waiting to hear the sound of gunfire—the sound that would signal the beginning of war in the Basin!

Miles sat in the swivel chair behind the solid oak desk in Major Barrow's office. The bank remained open until sundown on Saturdays, to accommodate the farmers and small ranchers who came to town only on weekends. It was almost sundown now, and he was growing impatient. It was possible Barrow would not return to the bank at all.

Miss Tinsey was getting ready to close. She had looked in on him twice, sniffing her disapproval.

Miles sat there, the thick stone walls insulating him from the sounds outside. It was quiet in the office, and seated behind the Major's big desk, with the picture of General Grant on the wall facing him and a battle scene of Shiloh in oil on the side wall, he seemed to be in another world, removed from Chuckline. A remote world, above local problems and impending violence.

Miles felt relaxed. He had cleaned up and shaved after leaving Ned Atwell's office and had had a quick meal at the lunchroom around the corner. Then, because he had come to town for this, he had returned to the bank.

He had just missed the arrival of Von Sesta with Cass and Breel; he was unaware of the

152

disturbance they had created, the quick shift in Brand's plans.

He heard the blinds being drawn in other windows outside the office, and after a few moments Miss Tinsey popped in again. She had her hat on.

'I'm closing up,' she said firmly. 'Elmer has already gone.'

Miles got to his feet. He would have preferred to see Major Barrow here—he did not like the idea of going to his home. What he had to say to John Barrow would not be pleasant . . .

Miss Tinsey drew back from the door as he walked toward her; she waited to close it behind him.

Miles grinned. 'Sorry to put you to this trouble, Miss Tinsey. Allow me to walk you home—'

The front door opened and Major Barrow entered. He came in quickly, turning to peer out for a moment before he closed it again. Whirling on his heel, he headed for the office with quick, harried strides. Then he saw Miles and Miss Tinsey and he stopped as though he had run into a stone wall.

Major Barrow leaned against the low barrier, a rumpled, impatient man. There was no dignity in him now. He seemed to choke at the sight of the tall boss of Hammer.

'Miles! What in the devil are you doing here?'

'Waiting for you. I want to talk to you—'

Barrow started to back-away. 'No! Not here! Not now!' He glanced wildly about the room, to the door. 'They're waiting out there! They're waiting to kill you!'

'*Who?*'

'Shaner and Von Sesta. Brand's killers!'

Miss Tinsey gasped. She started to sway, her face white. Miles stepped up to her, held her. 'Better sit down, Miss Tinsey,' he said gently.

'No!' Barrow's voice was harsh. 'Best to get her out of here!' He pushed through the gate in the railing, took her by the arm. 'You won't be harmed,' he said roughly.

He led to the door, opened it. 'Just walk away. Don't look back. Hurry!' He closed the door behind her, bolted it. He pulled the blind down over the glass pane and turned to Miles.

'They're saying you ambushed two of Ben Gaines' friends, that you killed Ben, too. Shaner and Von Sesta are looking for you. They're going to kill you, Miles—using the authority of the law to protect themselves!'

Miles' eyes narrowed.

'Shaner and Von Sesta? They're the men you had appointed to office, aren't they? That's why I came here, John. I want to know why.' His tone was bleak. 'I want to know why you forced the mayor and the commissioners to hire Brand's men!'

Barrow shook his head. 'They'll find out anyway,' he muttered. He seemed to be convincing himself. He was remembering that

Calvin Gammison had mentioned him in the wire to the United States Marshal's office. Barrow knew that a check-up would bring out the fact of his court-martial.

He walked back to the railing, blindly shoved through the low gate, sank down in Miss Tinsey's chair. He looked up at Miles, his face gray, a beaten look in his eyes.

'Brand blackmailed me,' he whispered. 'He forced me to back Shaner and Sesta. I had no alternative.'

Miles frowned. 'How? What is Brand to you?'

A sickly smile spread across Barrow's lips. 'Nothing. But to Brand I was a means to an end, a means to his getting Hammer.' He took a deep breath. 'He came to the Basin with that one purpose in mind, Miles—I know that now. He wants Hammer, wants it more than I've ever known any man to want anything. He wants to smash you—for some reason he hates you—'

He paused. In the deep silence a fly buzzed aimlessly. The sun's red stain against the windows was dying; it was growing dark in the bank.

'I made a mistake, a long time ago,' he muttered. 'I mislaid—' His lips tightened, and he met Miles' eyes, and some measure of dignity returned to him. He amended the statement he had started. 'I stole Army funds, Miles. I was found out during an audit of my

155

books and was court-martialed. I provided partial restitution and the board was lenient. However, I was drummed out of the service.' His voice stiffened. 'Kate knows nothing of this. She was living with my sister at the time—going to school in Philadelphia. Later, I came out here with her. I wanted to make a new start. I severed all connections with my old friends—'

His voice had dropped to a low murmur in the darkening room. Outside, it was strangely, ominously quiet.

'Somehow Brand found out about it,' he went on. 'The morning after Masters and Baldy were shot he came to see me. He put it bluntly. It was either go along with him concerning Shaner and Von Sesta, or he'd see to it the whole town would know they had a thief as their banker—'

'You knew what Brand wanted,' Miles cut in grimly. 'You knew then why he was set on their getting appointed as law officers?'

Barrow nodded. 'He told me. He wants Hammer. He even baited me with a promise of a share of it—' His lips twisted wryly. 'I think I never did lose that greed, Miles. I wanted money, power; wanted more than I have, even here.' His head sank on his chest. 'Now I have nothing—'

Miles let the silence spin out between them. There was little he could say to this man.

'Kate doesn't know,' the banker muttered.

He didn't raise his eyes. 'Whatever you think of me, I hope it doesn't change things between you.'

Miles considered. There was no point in hurting this man further; there would be time later for explanations. Kate would be happier with Ned Atwell, but Barrow would have to find this out for himself.

He said: 'I hold nothing against Kate, John.' He thought of Brand—of the men waiting for him outside. It was Brand's final play against Hammer.

Why? The question pounded in his head. He asked the man slumped in the chair.

The banker shook his head. 'He didn't tell me. But I think he knew your father once—hated him—'

Miles' lips tightened. 'It goes back to that then, John. I know it now. All this trouble goes back to my father—to his disappearance. I want you to do one thing for me. Whatever happens out there tonight, I want you to tell Gammison and the others about Brand, about Shaner and Sesta. Will you do that?'

Barrow took his time answering. Finally he nodded without speaking.

Miles turned away. At the front door he paused, checked his Colt. Then he drew back the bolt and stepped outside.

The closing door seemed to rouse Barrow to some decision he had been contemplating. He came to his feet and moved quickly to his office, to his desk. In the bottom drawer he kept a pearl-handled .38 caliber Smith and Wesson. He had been a good pistol shot once.

He checked it to assure himself it was loaded, then thrust it into his pocket. When he left the bank, it was by the back door, leading out to the narrow side street . . .

In the stillness of the darkening bank the fly still buzzed on its aimless quest.

CHAPTER SIXTEEN

Shaner and Von Sesta prowled the streets of Chuckline—they moved with the light, cautious stride of men on the kill, and the frightened citizens gave them passage. The word went out through Chuckline and the streets cleared as by magic; in the waning day the cowtown took on a deserted, unreal appearance.

Shaner walked with a long, restless stride. He wanted to get this over with. The thick envelope he had found in Masters' safe pressed against his bare stomach, reminding him of what waited for him up in the Dune country. He wanted to get away. But he knew he would have to go through with this thing first.

Von Sesta was across the street as he paused; the short, dark-faced killer came to

158

join him on the corner. At the point where they met the bank faced them, bulking square and solid on the far, opposite corner. The sun reflected a golden wash from its wide front windows.

Sesta rolled a smoke with the fingers of his left hand; his right was rock-steady as he cupped a match to it.

'He's hiding out somewhere, Red,' he muttered disappointedly. 'He must have got the word we're after him.'

Shaner's green eyes narrowed. He saw the teller come out of the bank, glance at them, and head off in the opposite direction. He shrugged. 'When I spotted him first he was headed for the bank. Could be he's still in there.'

He turned with the quick, easy movement of a hunting cat as a tall man came around the corner. His hand rested on his gun butt, then fell away.

Major Barrow glanced at them, lowered his head. He cut across the street toward the bank, lengthening his stride into a near-run.

'Wonder what's eating him?' Sesta growled.

Shaner rubbed his long jaw with the palm of his left hand. 'I've got a hunch, Von. Miles must be holed up in there.' He nodded toward the gray stone structure.

Sesta flipped his cigaret into the dust. 'Let's find out.' He stepped off the boardwalk and his boots kicked up little dust puffs as he headed for the bank.

The front door opened as he was in mid-street. An angular, sharp-faced woman appeared in the doorway; she seemed to be forcibly thrust out. The door closed abruptly behind her. The shade came down over the glass pane. The tip of the fading sun reflected from it, throwing its reddish barb across Sesta's path.

The woman turned and saw Sesta watching. She started to run along the boardwalk, and the little deputy took after her. He caught up to her before she had gone twenty feet, laid a rough hand on her shoulder and whirled her around.

'He's in there, ain't he?' he asked harshly. His face was thrust close to hers; she shrank back, her eyes closing. He repeated grimly: 'Miles North is in the bank, no?'

She nodded, her eyes still closed. He shoved her away and she tottered against the building.

Sesta ignored her. He arm-signaled Shaner to join him.

The sheriff came across the wide main street with long deliberate strides.

'He's in there all right.' Sesta grinned. 'Shall we wait, or go in and smoke him out?'

Shaner considered. 'We'll wait five minutes,' he decided. 'Then we'll go in after him!'

Sesta grinned. He moved back about twenty feet to the nearest awning support and leaned against it, like some lazy cat. From here he could watch the bank door, some forty yards away.

Shaner recrossed the street and moved swiftly along the far walk, cutting back to the corner where he had been joined by his deputy. He considered this vantage point briefly and decided against it. He crossed the street again, placing himself on the same side with the bank. The front door now lay between him and Von Sesta.

Shaner reached slowly in his shirt pocket for the makings, his eyes hard on that door. The sun was gone from the street. The sheriff's hands were steady as he rolled a quick smoke, put it between his lips.

He didn't get to light it!

*   *   *

The bank door opened and Miles North stepped out. It was a recessed door, and North, pausing for a survey of the street, was partially protected by the shouldering stone.

Shaner threw his unlighted cigaret away and stepped away from the building side.

Miles caught sight of the lanky sheriff first, some sixty yards away. Then Von Sesta's voice, calling sharply, turned him around.

'Over here, Miles,' the deputy said. His voice was pitched low, calculated to reach only as far as North—it rasped with thin, insolent challenge.

161

'Cut and draw, man!'

He wanted Miles to make his break. He didn't want the tall man to surrender peacefully. The deputy knew a hundred eyes were watching him, waiting to see how he handled this—and Sesta wanted Miles dead. If he could bait Miles into a shootout, the killing would have legal sanction.

Miles took one quick glance over his shoulder, and saw Shaner step off the walk into the street behind him. Whipsawed! For another long tense moment Miles kept to the protection of the doorway; in another few seconds Shaner would be at the right angle to cut down at him.

Sesta's voice came to him again, insulting, challenging. 'Afraid, Miles?'

He stepped away fast and cut down at Sesta as the little man drew with a swift motion. The two shots shattered the deadly quiet at almost the same moment.

Miles felt the shock of the bullet high in his left shoulder; the impact whirled him about and he dropped his Colt. He fell on it, fumbling to retrieve it, and Sesta's second shot went over him, painted a lead splotch on the stone wall and ricocheted off.

Von Sesta was standing on wide-spread legs, a strained, foolish look on his dark face. Miles slug had smashed into his middle; he had fallen back against the support and bounced forward again and thumbed that second wild

162

shot. Now he was straining to bring his Colt up again, straining to keep his feet while a shocked surprise began to twist his mouth.

Shaner broke into a run toward the bank. He didn't see the girl until she crossed his line of fire . . . His first shot missed Miles by a foot, splintered the boards in front of Hammer's boss. His second hit the girl . . .

Cobina stumbled, sprawled face down in front of the boardwalk.

It stopped the lanky sheriff. He had not intended to hit the girl; he had not even been aware she was about. He cursed grimly, looked around with a quick, apprehensive glance. The street was deserted, save for the girl in the road.

Miles had come to his feet. Sesta took one more shot at him as his knees began to buckle . . . the bullet went wild. Miles' return fire kicked Sesta around, sent him sprawling.

Shaner's panic grew. The affair was not going the way he had expected . . .

From the side street a .38 joined the fracas, its sharper bite riding the echoes of the .45's. Shaner hunched over, a surprised, hurt snarl crinkling his face. He turned to face the strange gun and saw Barrow standing close to the bank, holding a pistol. Barrow fired again, wildly now, as he realized Shaner had spotted him.

The sheriff's Colt blasted twice. Barrow fell back against the rough stones and slid down.

The Smith & Wesson slid from his limp grasp.

Miles had turned to face Shaner. His hand was unsteady and rage made him shoot wild. The sheriff was backing away, hunched over, seemingly hurt. Miles couldn't understand why; he was uncaring. He had seen Cobina cut across the street toward him; had seen her fall. She was lying a few feet in front of him, and he wanted to get the man who had shot her.

He set himself for another shot and Shaner's slug kicked his left foot from under him—he stumbled forward and drove into the porch support with his bullet-torn shoulder. The support cracked, and he caromed off it, and the excruciating pain upon impact blacked Miles out. He fell into the street.

In the stillness that settled over the darkening street Shaner kept backing away. Blood dyed his shirt front. His mouth was open, straining for air—his chest was on fire.

Far down the street a man opened up with a rifle. The slug kicked up dust near the sheriff's boots.

Shaner's eyes rolled wildly. He had to get away—he had finished his part of the job. Miles was dead. He was through here. He had to get to the Dune country—

A voice called sharply from behind him, 'Up here, Red!'

He turned and saw Brand ride out of an alley, leading a saddled horse. 'Hurry!' the man snapped.

Shaner holstered his Colt and stumbled to the horse. He grasped the horn and hung there a moment, gathering his fading strength. Brand was already whirling away, heading down the street.

The second rifle shot was uncomfortably close.

Shaner pulled himself into saddle. The big animal whirled, settled into a headlong run as Shaner raked his heels hard across his flanks.

He was three lengths behind Brand when they left town and cut across country for the far bulk of the Diamonds . . .

CHAPTER SEVENTEEN

The shadows crept in on the heels of the fading gunshots, and as a stunned silence returned men began moving out of doorways and alleys, converging toward the scene of the shooting.

Ned Atwell, a rifle in his hands, was the first to reach Miles and Cobina. Cobina was sitting up, staring blankly around her. The lawyer knelt beside her. He examined the tear under her right arm; blood made a dark stain down her side. But the angle of the bullet had caused it to cut a glancing blow, sliding off her ribs. It had knocked her out, but it wasn't serious.

She became aware of Miles' still form and a sob broke from her. She tried to stand up, but

Ned held her. 'You're in no condition to do anything, Cobina,' he said. He turned to the gathering crowd. 'Someone take her back to her father's office—I'll see how Miles is.'

Cobina struggled. 'No—I'm all right. I want to see Miles—'

Older men took her away. Atwell bent over Miles just as the boss of Hammer stirred. Ned's voice held a great relief. 'Give me a hand with him, boys. I think he isn't hurt too badly—'

Someone in the crowd said: 'Riders!' and the group scattered, moving toward the protection of the buildings.

Ned cuddled his rifle, turning to face the horsemen. He came to his feet just as Cud Walker pulled up in front of him. Behind Walker were a half-dozen Hammer riders.

Ned's face was grim. 'You're a few minutes too late,' he said, 'but in time to give me a hand with him—'

Walker's voice was like iron striking iron. 'What happened, Ned?'

'I'll tell you, in Doctor Kedner's office . . .'

*   *   *

A lot of things got straightened out in Kedner's crowded office. Breel, conscious and faced with angry men ready to string him to the nearest pole, talked. He told about Cass killing Jack Bevans and Lefty Conners—and Ben

166

Gaines. He told those men about Brand's determination to smash Hammer—and he cleared up the mystery of who had killed Baldy and Carl Masters.

'Red Shaner killed them,' he said. His voice was pitched low. 'The next day he an' Von Sesta were appointed as law officers.' He rolled his head. 'I don't know how Brand managed that—but it was his doing.'

Miles stood by the wounded man, his left shoulder bandaged. He asked the question which had plagued him since he had first suspected Brand was behind the trouble in the Basin.

'Why? Why did Brand come here in the first place? Why did he pick out Hammer?'

But Breel didn't know.

Ned Atwell was with Kate Barrow. John Barrow had been brought to the busy doctor, but he had died on the way. He had never recovered consciousness.

Mayor Gammison stood by helplessly as Ned comforted the Major's daughter. Cobina, her side bandaged, tried to help.

Miles turned to her. 'He saved my life, Kate.' His voice was tired. Major Barrow had paid a high price for his involuntary cooperation with Brand; the least he could do was to see that his secret died with him.

He turned to the door.

Mayor Gammison said: 'Where are you headed, Miles?'

167

The boss of Hammer grinned coldly. 'To the Flying B,' he said. 'Brand started this, Cal— Hammer guns will finish it!'

*   *   *

Shaner lasted as far as the foothills. He fought the slow drain on his strength to the last; in the end his will cracked and he slipped from the saddle, falling unconscious.

Brand, glancing back, saw him. He wheeled his cayuse and rode back to the man and dismounted. The Flying B was only a few more miles away; he could make it by daylight.

He glanced back into the night. If there had been any pursuit he had seen no sign of it.

He crouched beside the blood-soaked figure lying limp in the dust and turned him over. Shaner was still alive—he might pull through if he could get him to the spread. He had five men there—and the cook was a doctor of sorts.

He ripped Shaner's shirt away from the wound for a better look and the blood-stained envelope caught his attention. Frowning, he picked it up . . .

Minutes later he crammed the contents back into it and looked down at the man at his feet. His eyes were dark with a savage hate.

'How long have you had this?' he muttered. 'How long have you known?'

But Shaner was beyond listening.

Brand drew his Colt. He had come to smash

168

Hammer, and to retrieve what he felt was rightfully his. Farnum was dead—so was his son. And in view of what waited for him in the Dune country, Hammer no longer mattered.

Nor, he thought harshly, was his horse spread of any account.

He stepped back a few paces, and Shaner groaned. The redhead was struggling back to consciousness. He rolled over and tried to push himself up, but he never completely regained his senses.

Brand's Colt made a loud flat sound in the night. Shaner collapsed . . .

Brand went back to his horse, mounted. He took a last look at Shaner's body before he wheeled his cayuse away, turning him toward Saddle Pass.

*   *   *

The Hammer riders came across Shaner's body just before dawn. Miles and Walker examined the body. It was the old foreman, an expert tracker, who read what had happened there.

'Looks like Shaner fell off his cayuse and Brand rode back for him. Whatever made him decide to do it, he killed Shaner and changed his mind about heading for his horse spread. From here I'd say he's heading for Saddle Pass—'

Miles nodded grimly. 'Brand's my man,' he

169

muttered. 'You take the boys up to the Flying B. If they hold out, wipe them out!'

Walker shrugged. 'He's got an hour's start on you, Miles.'

'I'm betting on Mig here,' Miles said. He stroked the big black's neck. 'I think we can run him down, Cud—if we have to ride to the end of the earth to do it!'

The Dune country wasn't the end of the earth, but it was close to it. Miles caught up to Brand at the end of the long day. The big black was spent.

The hills of sand ran like tawny frozen waves beneath the blazing sun, making footing treacherous. Brand's trail skirted these hills, keeping to the hard, broken ground swept bare by southern winds.

Brand was digging at the foot of a gnarled, ancient oak when Miles came into sight. He was using his Colt muzzle to loosen the hard earth, digging with his hands.

He heard his horse snort behind him and he brought his head up. He saw Miles come into view less than a hundred yards away.

For one dragging moment Brand stared at this man he had thought dead. Then he came to his feet and tried to use his Colt.

Packed earth jammed the cylinder. Panic rode roughshod over his common sense; he dropped the Colt and jumped for his ground-reined cayuse, clawing for his rifle.

He had it free and turned it on Miles—he

managed to get in one shot before Miles' Colt beat him back. He fell against his cayuse and the animal moved away, startled by the gunfire. Brand fell at the horse's feet. He fell in a sitting position, his eyes glazed . . . He had his rifle still in his possession and instinctively worked his hands. He levered a shell into position and raised the muzzle toward the man riding down on him.

The sharp spang blended with the heavier blast from Miles' gun, and Brand fell back as though shoved by a giant hand . . .

*   *   *

Wearily Miles North knelt beside the dead man. Now that Brand was dead, it seemed likely he would never know what had brought him here.

The blood-stained envelope sticking up from Brand's coat pocket caught his attention He picked it up, opened it; read through the now dog-eared, thumb-stained pages of his father's letter.

'When you get this letter, son,' the note began, 'I will be dead. Wyeth Brand will have killed me. I write this advisedly, for in the unlikely chance that I can talk Brand into understanding, that I can convince him I had nothing to do with his going to prison, you will never receive this letter.

'But I am afraid Brand will not listen to

171

reason.

'First, read the enclosed clipping. Brand sent it to me a few days ago, enclosed in the letter asking me to meet him in the Dune country. The clipping will partially explain what happened . . .'

Miles turned to the yellow newspaper clipping. The date-line was nearly twenty years old.

MORE THAN ONE HUNDRED THOUSAND DOLLARS STOLEN IN DARING TRAIN ROBBERY.

That was the headline. The story under it went on in detail about the robbery by three masked men.

'Wyeth Brand, myself and Big Al Moseby were those holdup men,' his father's letter continued. 'One hundred and thirty thousand dollars was in that haul, son.

'Pursuit was close. I was carrying the money. In the night we got separated. I never saw Big Al or Brand again. But I read later, where Al got killed by the posse which ran him down. And it wasn't until four months later that Brand was picked up, tried, and sentenced to twenty years.

'I think he must have gone crazy in prison, thinking of the money. He began to believe I had given him away, tipped off the law. But he never gave me away. I think he must have decided then that he would eventually get out—that he would have his share, and mine, when he did.

'I have few excuses for what I did, son. It was my first and only venture into anything like that and the rewards were fantastically high.

'For years I had kept writing to your mother that I would strike it rich. This time I had, but I was ashamed to tell her how I had come into the money. I had one hundred and thirty thousand dollars and I didn't know how to use it.

'I was headed south, for Mexico, when I drifted through the Dune country, through Saddle Pass and into the Basin. It was virgin range, and it was then I saw the possibilities ahead.

'I started Hammer with stolen money, son. I was desperate to have you and your mother with me again. I wanted to give your mother everything she had ever wanted; I wanted to give you a better start than I had had.

'But that money dragged on me. I buried most of it (you'll find where I hid it in the map at the end of this letter). I used less than thirty thousand dollars to start Hammer. I never went back for more. I intended always to make full restitution, but I never got up the courage.

'I forgot about Brand until his letter arrived. I know what he wants, son—what he considers his share. Possibly he'll want all of it. I shall try to talk him out of it. I don't think I'll succeed.

'But whatever happens, son, don't let him take Hammer. Over the years I have managed to put back the thirty thousand I used to start the ranch. That money is in the Dune country, waiting for you. I want you to do with it what I never did—return it.

A breeze fluttered the pages in Miles' hand. He stood unseeing now, remembering his father as he had last seen him.

No one in the Basin had ever suspected that Farnum North was anything but an honest, hard-working man. That would be the way they would remember him.

He turned to the oak where Brand had been digging. He would see that the money was returned—anonymously.

*　　　*　　　*

Two days later Harry Kedner opened the door to him. Miles came into the room, his hat in his hand. He said quietly: 'I've come to see Cobina.'

Kedner nodded. 'She's in the living room. She wasn't badly hurt, Miles—'

But Miles was already turning away from him. He found Cobina reading, curled up in a big chair. She looked up as he came to her. Her eyes lighted. 'Miles—'

He stopped by her side. He had a lot of things to say to her, but the look in her eyes told him they could wait. He said slowly:

'Young lady, I think you need a doctor—' and bent down to her, to her eager, waiting lips.

Behind him Doctor Kedner closed the door and turned back to his office, whistling softly . . .

We hope you have enjoyed this Large Print book. Other Chivers Press or G.K. Hall & Co. Large Print books are available at your library or directly from the publishers.

For more information about current and forthcoming titles, please call or write, without obligation, to:

Chivers Press Limited
Windsor Bridge Road
Bath BA2 3AX
England
Tel. (01225) 335336

OR

G.K. Hall & Co.
P.O. Box 159
Thorndike, Maine 04986
USA
Tel. (800) 223-2336

All our Large Print titles are designed for easy reading, and all our books are made to last.